Madison Sampso

Only

the

Spy

a l l y   c a r t e r

SCHOLASTIC INC.
New York Toronto London Auckland
Sydney Mexico City New Delhi Hong Kong

ISBN 978-0-545-44925-0

Copyright © 2010 by Ally Carter.
All rights reserved. Published by Scholastic Inc., 557 Broadway, New York, NY 10012, by arrangement with Hyperion Books for Children, an imprint of Disney Book Group, LLC. SCHOLASTIC and associated logos are trademarks and/or registered trademarks of Scholastic Inc.

12 11 10 9 8 7 6 5 4 3 2 1   12 13 14 15 16 17/0

Printed in the U.S.A.   40

This edition first printing, February 2012

This book is set in Goudy.

For Daddy

Chapter One

"Targets acquired, ten o'clock."

My best friend's voice was as cool as the wind as it blew off the Thames. Her resolve was as solid as the Tower of London's ancient stone walls that stood twenty feet away. I could see the night getting darker—the lights grow brighter—and my best friend's confidence was almost contagious. *Almost*. But staring at the crowd in the distance, I couldn't help but think *I am not prepared for this.*

I mean, don't get me wrong, I am prepared for *a lot* of scary situations. After all, in the last year and a half I'd been fake kidnapped once, almost truly kidnapped twice, targeted by one international terrorist organization and two incredibly cute boys. So, scary? Yeah, scary and I go *way* back.

But at that moment Rebecca Baxter and I were standing on ice skates on a rink that used to be the moat around the Tower of London. We were outnumbered and outsized. So something about that moment was . . . terrifying.

Even though my best friend was beside me. Even though our school had trained us well.

Even though we go to a school for spies.

"Ooh, Cam. They're looking this way."

Part of me hoped Bex was talking about her father, who stood by the skating rink's concession stand, or her mother, who was by the rink's east exit. I totally wished that Bex was talking about the agents in the crowd, whose job it was to protect me—like the woman with the backpack who had been trailing us all afternoon, or the man who was posted at the top of Tower Bridge, as it spanned the Thames and offered a birds'-eye view of all transportation routes for a half mile in any direction. But I knew Rebecca Baxter well enough to know that she wasn't talking about the spies. She was talking about . . . the boys.

When Bex spun effortlessly and skated backward past the crowd of guys that stood laughing and showing off at the edge of the rink, every single one of them turned to stare at her. Her red scarf waved in the wind as she smiled. "So which one do you want?"

"No thanks." I shrugged. "Trying to give them up."

I mean, sure, they *looked* nice, cute, and completely harmless, but if there's one thing we Gallagher Girls know, it's that looks can totally be deceiving.

"Come on, Cam," Bex pleaded. "How about the tall one?"

"Nope."

"The short one?"

"No thank you," I said with a shake of my head.

"The one with..." Bex didn't finish. Her eyes went wide and she stared past me, but my mind was thinking back to a chilly November night in Washington, D.C., and a steamy summer afternoon on a rooftop in Boston, as the two scariest moments of my life flashed before my eyes.

I felt my heart begin to pound. "What is it?" I scanned the crowd, trying to catch a glimpse of what Bex had seen.

"Cam..." Bex started.

I spun around on the ice, waiting for Bex's mother, for her father, for some of my guards to register the same shock I saw in my best friend's eyes, but their faces were blank.

"Bex," I snapped, "what is it?"

"It's nothing. It's just...Tell me this, Cam..." Her smile was pure evil, and she spoke so slowly that I sort of wanted to hurt her. "Just tell me...are you sure you've given up *all* boys?"

"Bex, what are you saying?" I asked.

But my best friend just pouted, raised her hand to her mouth, and said, "*Oops.*"

And then Rebecca Baxter, the most highly coordinated girl at the Gallagher Academy for Exceptional Young Women (which, believe me, includes some *really* coordinated girls), tumbled onto the ice.

Well, it turns out that pretending to fall down is an excellent way to make boys stop staring and start moving. Of course, our other roommate, Liz, would no doubt require a lot more evidence before citing that as a scientific certainty, but considering the fact that eight boys had been staring and seven boys rushed to Bex's rescue, I'd say our results were pretty statistically sound.

But, honestly, at that moment statistics were the last thing on my mind, because fluffy white snowflakes were floating through the night sky that stood between me and the one boy who didn't move, the boy who didn't swoon, the boy who just stood by the rails with his hands in his pockets, staring at me, saying, "Happy New Year, Gallagher Girl."

There is a pretty wide range of emotions that any girl—much less a Gallagher Girl—is bound to encounter on any given day —from joy to sadness, frustration to excitement.

At that moment it's pretty safe to say that I was feeling all of them.

And I was trying to show none of them.

Bex's seven suitors kneeled beside her on the ice, while my skates pulled me closer to the one boy who lingered by the rail.

"You look cold," I somehow managed to say.

"I used to have a warmer jacket, but then I gave it to some girl."

"That wasn't very smart."

"No." He smirked and shook his head. "It probably wasn't."

Despite having known him for almost a year, there were *a lot* of things I still didn't know about Zachary Goode. Like how soap and shampoo could smell so much better on him than anyone else. Like where he went when he wasn't mysteriously showing up at random (and frequently dangerous) points in my life. And, most of all, I didn't know how, when he mentioned the jacket, he made me think about the sweet, romantic part of the night last November when he'd given it to me, and not the terrible, bloody, international-terrorists-are-trying-to-kidnap-me part that came right after.

From the corner of my eye, I could see that the boys had "helped" Bex to a bench not far away, but Zach didn't seem to notice. He just inched closer to me and smiled.

"Besides, it looked better on you."

There are a lot of things that the Gallagher Academy teaches us to remember, but right then I was wishing my exceptional education had also taught me how to forget.

I mean, it was a chilly night in a foreign city, and an incredibly hot boy was smiling at me through the soft glow of sparkly lights! The absolute last thing I wanted to remember was the last time I'd seen Zach—the screeching tires or the masked men. Seriously, forgetting would have come in so incredibly handy at that particular moment. But I'm a Gallagher Girl. We don't forget anything.

"Why do I get the feeling you aren't here on vacation?" I asked.

I heard Bex laughing. I sensed Zach's hand inching down the rail, closer and closer to mine. For just one second, I thought he might say *me*—that he was here to see me.

"I'm looking for Joe Solomon." He glanced around the Tower grounds. "Thought maybe he was with you?"

And just that quickly the pounding of my heart took on an entirely different meaning. Sure, it sounded like an easy question, but nothing about my Covert Operations instructor has ever been easy. Ever.

"What's wrong?" I asked, my mind reeling with at least a

dozen reasons why Mr. Solomon might follow me to London —and not one of them was good.

"Nothing, Gallagher Girl. It's probably noth—"

"Tell me or I'll yell for Mr. and Mrs. Baxter, and you can find out how Bex became *Bex*."

He kicked at the hard-packed snow gathered at the edge of the rink.

"We were supposed to meet up a few days ago, but he didn't show." Zach stared at me. "And he didn't call."

Okay, I know when most teenagers talk about someone not calling, they're usually complaining. Or whining. But Zach isn't exactly the whining type.

I felt cold for the first time on the ice.

"He's not on my protection detail."

"Your mom's off looking for leads on the Circle, right?" Zach asked. "Could he be with her?"

"I don't know," I said. "I *guess* so, but...I don't know."

"Has he checked in with the Baxters?"

"I don't know."

"Has he—"

"No one ever tells me anything, remember?" I searched his face, and despite everything, I couldn't help but savor the fact that there was finally something Zach didn't know. "Being out of the loop isn't fun, is it?"

"Rebecca!" Bex's mother's voice echoed through the cold air.

"You've got to go," Zach said with a nod in the Baxters' direction.

"If Mr. Solomon is missing call-ins, then we have to look for him. We've got to tell Bex's parents. . . . We've got to call my mom so she can—"

"No," Zach snapped, then shook his head and forced a smile. "It's probably nothing, Gallagher Girl. Go on. Have fun," he said, as if that were possible.

"Cameron," Bex's father called. "Say good-bye to the young man now."

"We've got to tell them, Zach. If Mr. Solomon is missing . . ."

"They'd know," Zach reminded me. His voice softened. "Whatever is going on, I promise you they know a lot more than we do."

Zach eased away from the rail while, behind us, Mr. Baxter's voice grew louder. "Let's go, Cammie!"

I looked over my shoulder at my best friend's father, her mother, and the guards that had surrounded me for weeks. "I'll be right there!"

When I turned back to the rail, Zach was already gone.

Chapter two

Bex's dad is one of England's top spies (not to mention the man who taught his daughter how to use Barbie as a weapon when she was seven), so I didn't run after Zach. I didn't yell. I just kept pace beside Abe Baxter, skating slowly across the ice.

"The Tower of London is the oldest royal building still in official use today, Cammie."

"She knows, Dad," Bex said, even though A) I actually *didn't* know, and B) at that point, I had far more covert facts on my mind.

"Mr. Baxter—" I started, but Bex's father was already pointing at the Tower's tall stone walls and saying, "The Jewel House alone is a Grade AA target—"

"She knows, Dad," Bex said again, rolling her eyes. But she didn't really seem annoyed when she stared up at her father, listening for him to go on.

"It has reinforced titanium security gates and a nine-hundred-and-eighty-point self-modifying laser grid." Then he stopped. "I'm sorry, Cammie, you were saying?"

But something in the way he looked at me made me forget about Zach and Mr. Solomon and even the Circle of Cavan. Something reminded me that dads tell corny jokes. Dads drone on and on about history and facts that don't really matter to ninety-nine percent of the world's population. Dads sometimes look at daughters like they're more precious than all the diamonds in England. I remembered that—once upon a time—someone had looked like that at me.

"I . . . I just wanted to thank you again for letting me spend winter break with you," I managed to mutter.

He squeezed my shoulder. "It's our pleasure, Cameron."

And just like that, I told myself that Zach was right—it was probably nothing. Everything was probably fine. After all, Mr. Solomon was careful. Mr. Solomon was good.

Still, as I glided to one of the benches and started loosening the laces on my skates, my fingers didn't want to work. It was like I'd forgotten how to breathe.

"Ooh . . . ravens!" Mr. Baxter said, easing onto the bench beside me. He pointed to a blackbird that was scavenging for crumbs near the base of the tall stone wall. "Now, there's an interesting piece of history, Cammie. According to legend, England will fall if the ravens ever leave the Tower of London."

I looked at the bird but didn't say anything. It was so black against the white ice.

Mr. Baxter sighed. "They clip their wings so they can't fly away."

And then, despite the icy wind, my face felt hot. My hands were sweating inside my gloves while I pulled at the scarf around my neck, suddenly dizzy as I stood in my socks on the frozen ground, while the skaters kept circling around and around.

Mr. Baxter stood. "What is it, Cammie? What's wrong?"

I shook my head. "It's . . . nothing."

But something was coming over me—like déjà vu, only stronger. There was something in the crowd that I should know, something I should see. I shook my head, and for a split second I thought I saw a tall, graceful woman across the ice; my breath caught as I remembered the woman from the rooftop in Boston.

"No," I muttered.

I looked at Mrs. Baxter and her colleague with the backpack who had been following us all day. They each held cups of coffee in their right hands—the sign that our tail was clear, that things were fine. But things weren't fine. There was a ghost in that crowd—something I should see. Something I should know.

"Cammie?" Mr. Baxter's hand was on my shoulder. "What is it?"

"I don't know." I shook my head. "It's just—"

Before I could finish, I heard a burst of static from the comms unit in Mr. Baxter's ear—a distant, muffled cry. Across the ice, the woman with the backpack spun, as if looking for something—someone. The cup fell from her hand and tumbled toward the ice. And in that moment, my mind flashed back to D.C., and then further back, to Boston.

Get her. The words echoed in my mind.

Get me.

And then the lights went out.

Chapter tHReE

Even in the pitch blackness, I knew that commands were ringing in the ears of the agents at the rink. In an instant, Mr. Baxter grabbed me, pulling me away from the ice and closer to the shelter of the Tower's stone walls.

The ground was hard and cold against my feet, but there was no time to grab my boots—not a second to do anything but run and listen to the cries that floated through the dark. I kept one hand against the rough stone wall and the other tightly in Mr. Baxter's grasp as we moved deeper into the crowd of panicking tourists—pushing through the chaos—until, suddenly, Mr. Baxter's hand pulled free of mine.

"Cammie!" he yelled, and I reached for him through the dark, but there were too many people.

"Cammie!" he called again, but before I could answer, a pair of strong arms locked around my waist, and someone pinned me against the stone wall. I started to strike out, but the man countered as if he'd known exactly what I'd been trained to do. He squeezed my arms to my sides so tightly that I only had one choice: I pulled my head back and struck with all my might. I felt the blow land—heard the man wince. Then something else—a familiar voice in my ear, saying, "Cammie, calm down."

For a second I thought I must be wearing a comms unit —that my teacher's voice was coming back to me, telling me how to save my own life.

"Cammie, stop fighting," the voice whispered as, one by one, the Tower's backup security lights began to flicker to life. And through the soft glow that spread over the grounds, I saw Joe Solomon staring into my eyes. I felt him grab my hand.

And I heard him whisper, "*Run.*"

"They're coming, aren't they?" My breath fogged in the cold air, and yet my arms kept pumping, my feet kept moving, and my teacher kept a solid grip on my hand, pulling me across the Tower's dim grounds toward a busy London street while I said the words I'd been dreading for weeks:

"The Circle . . . they're here."

"Ms. Morgan, we only have a minute until they find us, so you have to listen to me very carefully," my teacher said, tightening his hold on my hand, urging me through the steady stream of traffic and onto Tower Bridge.

"Are you on comms? You have to tell the Baxters you have me. We have to call in an extraction team and—"

"Cammie, listen!" His order seemed to echo in the dark, and something about it made me stop there in the middle of the bridge. He sounded angry and frantic and scared.

Joe Solomon was scared.

He grabbed me by both shoulders. "Cammie, we only have a minute until they find us, and then they'll take you away—"

"No!" I shouted.

"Listen! Any day now they're going to take you back to school, and when you get there, you have to—"

"Hello, Joe."

When Bex's father appeared on the dark bank of the river, his voice was even and calm, but he wore the same expression that Bex does when she's focused and angry and when there's no force on earth that can stop her.

And yet Mr. Solomon didn't turn to look at him. He was still gripping my shoulders as if no assignment in my entire life had ever been more important than the one he was about to give. "Cammie, listen to me!"

"Come on, Joe," Mr. Baxter called across the bridge, easing forward like a man bracing for a fight. "Turn yourself in. Let the girl go."

I shook my head. Nothing made sense in that moment—not what Mr. Solomon was saying or the way Mr. Baxter was looking at us. Neither of them seemed to know that they were both on the same side—my side.

"It's okay, Mr. Baxter," I said, turning to Bex's father, thinking maybe he didn't recognize my teacher. "This is Mr. Solomon. *Joe Solomon*. He's—"

"I know who he is, Cammie." Bex's father inched closer. "And he's going to come with me now—fly to Langley and get this mess straightened out."

14

"Cammie!" Mr. Solomon shook me slightly. "Don't listen to him. Listen to me!"

But Bex's father kept talking. "Joe, you've got to let her go."

Bex's mother walked out of the shadows behind her husband. "Cammie, sweetheart, I want you to walk over to me now."

The bridge was cold and rough beneath my feet, but I didn't move. I scanned the shadowy banks of the river, looking for Bex, needing her to help me explain to her parents that they were making a terrible mistake. But all I saw were guards and operatives who were closing ranks around us, and in that moment I realized that no one was searching the crowd. Not a soul was looking for the Circle. Instead, the people who had sworn to protect me were staring as if that bridge were the most dangerous place in the world that I could be.

When the operative from the observation tower appeared on the opposite end of the bridge, I knew we were surrounded.

"Cammie, now!" Mrs. Baxter ordered, but I stayed frozen in place.

"Her father was my best friend!" my teacher shouted, the words echoing off the river and out into the night.

Bex's father nodded and eased closer. "I know."

"This is crazy, Abe." Mr. Solomon shook his head.

"Sure it is," Mr. Baxter said calmly. "But protocols exist for a reason, Joe. We know—"

"We know how this ends!" my teacher shouted.

"Not this time," Mr. Baxter said. "Not necessarily. Not if you let Cammie go, and come with me."

"Mr. Solomon . . ." I didn't recognize my own voice. It

sounded far off and frail. I saw the way I stayed in the shadows, not fighting against my teacher's grasp. Weak. I felt weak. And so I pulled away.

"Cammie, come here," Bex's mom ordered again. I could see Bex behind her, not moving. Dazed. "Cammie!" Bex's mom snapped, but I looked at my teacher.

"Mr. Solomon, what is going on? Why are you here? Why didn't you meet Zach? Why do they keep looking at you like . . . Why are they talking like *you're* the enemy?"

"The CIA has some questions for him, Cammie," Mr. Baxter answered. "That's all. He just needs to answer some questions."

"You're gonna try to turn me in, Abe?" Mr. Solomon laughed, then turned to Bex's mom. "Grace? Are you going to cuff me in front of Bex and Cammie?"

Bex cried, "No!" but her mother's voice was even as she said, "You know we have to."

"Mom!" Bex cried.

"Rebecca, stay out of this," Bex's father warned. Then he looked at the man we all knew—the man only Bex and I still trusted. "You should have known better than to come here, Joe."

"I had to talk to Cammie."

"Cammie was safe with us," Bex's mother told him.

My teacher just shook his head. "Cammie isn't safe *anywhere*."

I didn't want to cry then, but I couldn't pretend anymore either. I wasn't on vacation. I was hiding. I was like the ravens, a prisoner of a destiny I didn't know and couldn't control. So

I looked at the grown-up I knew best—the only man I'd truly trusted in a very long time.

"Mr. Solomon, please, what's going on?"

And then his hands were back on my shoulders. "Cammie, you have to follow the pigeons."

"I . . . I don't understand."

"Promise me, Cammie! No matter what, promise me you will *follow the pigeons*."

It didn't make any sense—not the words or the look in his eyes or the way my best friend's parents stood staring as if the moment they'd been dreading for days was finally here.

A siren sounded, and I felt suddenly unsteady on my feet, as if the earth were moving.

"Mr. Solomon," I spoke slowly, calmly, "maybe you *should* come with us. . . . We'll call my mom and she'll explain that you're a teacher and that there's been some kind of mistake and . . ."

But then I couldn't finish because the earth *was* moving. The siren was growing louder; spectators were beginning to call out from the riverbanks. In a terrible flash, I remembered that Tower Bridge is a *drawbridge*, and Mr. Solomon and I were standing in the center.

The bridge lurched and Bex yelled, "Cammie!" but her mother held her back.

I grabbed at the rail as the bridge rose higher and steeper, and Mr. Solomon reached for my shoulders, holding me, steadying me.

"Cammie, you have to *promise me!*"

"Okay, Mr. Solomon. Of course. I promise."

"Thank you, Cammie." He relaxed his grip and lowered his head. For the first time, he seemed to breathe as he sighed, "Thank you."

"Okay, Joe." Mr. Baxter inched closer. "You talked to Cammie. You got your promise. Now, come on. Let's go get this settled."

But Mr. Solomon was backing away, his gaze still locked on me.

"The pigeons, Cammie."

"The pigeons," I said.

And then one of the greatest spies I've ever known ran toward the rising edge of the bridge and propelled himself over the top, flying, falling. Bex's parents rushed after him, but I was already there, staring into the Thames.

And Joe Solomon was already gone.

Chapter foUR

During winter break of our seventh-grade year, Bex helped her parents expose a double agent who had been working inside MI6. The summer she turned fourteen she swears she disabled a bomb beneath the royal family's box in the bleachers at Wimbledon. But as Bex and I sat in the back of an MI6 van with the words "Handy Helpers House Painting Service" painted on the side, I knew no Gallagher Girl had ever brought a story quite like this one home from school vacation.

I tried recounting the facts for myself—how the first agent to reach us was left-handed and had green eyes, how the phone number on the side of the van had a Surrey exchange. I remembered all the details—every single one. After all, Mr. Solomon had trained me well. And that was the problem, really.

Mr. Solomon had trained me.

Mr. Solomon had taught me.

And then Mr. Solomon had dragged me onto that bridge and jumped into the cold, dark waters of the Thames. So I sat quietly with Mr. Baxter on one side of me, and Mrs. Baxter on the other, waiting for the world to stop spinning in the wrong direction.

But, of course, for all of Rebecca Baxter's talents, *waiting* totally isn't one of them.

"*What was that?*" Bex exclaimed as soon as the van doors slammed.

"Quiet, Rebecca," her mother ordered.

"Because it looked like the two of you just tried to *arrest* Joe Solomon," Bex said. "Is that what it looked like to you, Cam?"

"Not now, Rebecca," her father said.

"So what was that, then?" Bex asked. "Training op?"

"Bex," her mother hissed.

"Perimeter security test?" Bex tried.

"Rebecca, I will have that agent pull this van over," her father warned, but Bex just plowed on.

"Because, correct me if I'm wrong, but isn't Joe Solomon one of the *good* guys?"

I wish her parents had cut her off, scolded her, said something—anything—because nothing could have been scarier than the look that passed between Mr. and Mrs. Baxter just then. Even Bex went quiet at the sight.

A minute later I felt the van veer and slow and, all around us, the world got dark. Through the van's interior light, Bex looked at me. "Tunnel?" I guessed.

She stared at me and whispered back, "Zach?"

Before I could answer, the tunnel lights flickered, and we

were lost in total darkness as the driver yanked the wheel. Tires screeched. I grabbed on to the seat, felt the swerve of the Baxters on either side of me, and yet no one screamed or braced for a crash as we careened fast—too fast—toward the tunnel wall. In the darkness I felt my best friend's hand reach out and grasp my own, as suddenly, the wall in front of us parted, and the painter's van was swallowed up whole.

I spun in my seat, and through the van's dusty rear windows I saw the hidden door close.

"Cool," Bex whispered.

Then there was a light at the end of the tunnel (*literally*). Everything grew brighter while the van slowed and the passage grew wider until the space we were in was anything but a tunnel anymore.

"Welcome to Baring Cross Station," a high voice said as the van door slid open.

Instantly, Bex's mother's arm was around my waist; her father's hand was gripping mine, and the best and brightest of Her Majesty's Secret Service were staring, watching me climb out of the van as if *I* were the most interesting thing in that cavernous space.

The ceiling must have been five stories high. Catwalks sprawled above, and more vans sat to my right, parked at strange angles. All around us, people ran, shouting orders. There were stainless-steel staircases, polished chrome risers and frosted-glass partitions everywhere. I couldn't help but think that it had been almost exactly a year since I'd been escorted into another super-cool, super-secret underground facility in a major world capital.

But my trip to the secret facility beneath D.C. had been because of a boy. (Or ... more specifically ... a *boyfriend*.) In London, it was because of a man. (Or ... more specifically ... a *teacher*.) The year before, I'd known the trip was coming. This time nothing about the day was in any way routine. Last winter, my mother had taken me to that facility to answer questions. But this time I stood beside the Baxters, consumed by the things I didn't know.

"Are you okay?" a woman asked.

"Did he hurt you?" a man with surgical gloves and a white coat wanted to know.

"How the bloody hell did he get so close?" another man snapped.

"Traitor's Gate," one of the women answered. "He came in through Traitor's Gate."

"Of course he did," the man mumbled, and I tried to shake the words from my head. They were gibberish. Nonsense. Because "he" was Mr. Solomon.

"He" was one of the best spies I've ever known.

"He" was my father's best friend.

As we walked past a massive wall of screens, images of the city flashed by so quickly it was a miracle anyone could see a thing.

"Satellite is up!" a young man in horn-rimmed glasses yelled.

"Get me eyes on every tube entrance, every intersection, every airport. We're close, people!" an older woman cried. "Let's not let him get away."

Bex's eyes found mine, and I knew what she was thinking: our teacher wouldn't have walked onto that bridge if he hadn't had a way of getting off; he wouldn't have come to London if he hadn't had a way of getting out; and when Joe Solomon doesn't want to be found, there's not a camera, satellite, or operative on earth who can see him.

"Baxter!" a voice called from the catwalk above us. "You have the girl, then?"

Bex's father placed his arm around my shoulder. "She's here. She's fine."

The man gestured to a metal door at the end of the catwalk. "Then come this way," he told me, but Bex stepped closer.

"We'll be happy to wait in there," she said.

The agent looked at Mrs. Baxter, whose face was just as determined as her daughter's.

"I'm going with her," Mrs. Baxter said. "Cammie is our responsibility."

"Then you should have thought about that before you took her bloody ice skating," the agent snapped.

I wanted to say something in protest—to remind them that it wasn't the Baxters' fault—whatever "it" was. But Mrs. Baxter's hand was on my shoulder, gently pushing me forward, telling me that the path I was on now was one I had to walk alone.

Chapter five

PROS AND CONS OF SPENDING THE NIGHT
IN A TOP SECRET ROOM OF A TOP SECRET
FACILITY, BUT NO ONE WILL TELL YOU WHY:
(A list by Cameron Morgan)

PRO: Turns out, top secret underground government facilities are an excellent place to warm up after ice skating.

CON: The warming-up process includes no friends, no family, and absolutely no answers.

PRO: Sometimes it's nice having a moment alone to compose yourself after fairly traumatic (and totally confusing) experiences.

CON: The "moment" stops being nice when it goes on for almost two hours.

PRO: Three words—Extra. Credit. Essay.

CON: Two words—No. Bathroom.

PRO: Knowing there are fifty operatives and at least two hundred cameras between you and the people trying to get you.

CON: Realizing you know even less about those people than you thought you did. A lot less.

———————

Every good operative knows there are several reasons to keep someone waiting before questioning them. Sometimes you want to make them nervous; sometimes you want to let them think; sometimes you need to gather the facts; and sometimes talking to them just isn't that important. But there was only one reason that occurred to me when I heard the door creak open and pulled my head and arms off of the cold steel table.

"Is my mother here?"

"No."

The door slammed, and I turned to watch a man I'd never seen before walk to the other side of the room. He was tall with black wavy hair and deep blue eyes, and as he spoke in his rich British accent, both the spy in me and the girl in me became instantly aware of the fact that I was drooling.

"How are you, Cammie?" he asked, but barely waited to hear my "Fine."

"Is there anything you need? Water? Something to—"

"What happened on the bridge?"

The man chuckled softly. "Well, that's what I was hoping you could tell me." He dropped a file onto the table between us and moved to the chair opposite mine, but there was something about the gesture—the sound of his laugh—that felt strange to me. Nothing seemed that funny anymore.

"He didn't hurt you?" the man asked.

"Mr. Solomon is my teacher. He would never hurt me."

"Are you *sure* we can't get you something? Some hot cocoa, maybe?"

"I don't want cocoa. I want to know why a six-person grab team just surrounded Joe Solomon. I want to know why one of the CIA's best operatives had to break me out of MI6's protection to talk to me. I mean, we *are* on the same side, aren't we?"

And then the man's smile disappeared—faded in a flash. "Oh, we know who our friends are."

"Really? Because it seems—"

"What happened on the bridge?"

"That's what I'm asking *you*."

"What did Joe Solomon *say* on the bridge?" He gritted his teeth as he reworded his question.

"I don't know. It all happened so fast. I didn't really understand."

Again he laughed, and this time mumbled, "Of course you didn't."

"What's your name?" I asked, but he didn't answer. "You're MI6, right?"

"Impressive," he said, but something in his tone told me he wasn't impressed at all.

"Who are you? Where are the Baxters?"

He shifted in his seat and leaned forward. "Thanks to the

Baxters, half of London saw what happened today, which, in our business, is a *bad* thing. So the Baxters are a little tied up at the moment."

I didn't know what was worse, that Bex's parents were in trouble because of me, or that the man across from me was talking to me like I was an outsider—a fraud. Sure, I *am* a sixteen-year-old-girl-slash-operative-in-training, and, don't get me wrong, the sixteen-year-old-girl part has come in seriously handy on occasion, but he was giving me the kind of look I've come to expect from people who don't know the truth about my school —and the man across from me *was supposed* to know the truth.

At least I thought he was.

"Um . . . just out of curiosity," I said, "what level of clearance do you have?"

"What level of clearance do *you* have?"

"I asked you first."

The man smirked, then said, "High enough." Which wasn't really an answer, but I didn't think this was the time to say so.

"Why is everyone looking for Mr. Solomon?" I asked. When the man leaned back in his chair, I leaned closer and searched his blue eyes. "There's been some kind of mistake," I told him. "Call the Gallagher Academy. Call my mother."

"What did Joe Solomon tell you on the bridge?" the man snapped, but I barely heard the words.

"My mother is Rachel Morgan, operative ID 145-23-6741. Headmistress of the Gallagher Academy for Exceptional Young Women. You have to—"

"I know who your mother is," he stated calmly. "Now tell me about Joe Solomon!"

I let the words wash over me, tried to find the center of my rage, of my fear, before I slowly whispered, "The pigeons. Mr. Solomon told me to follow the pigeons."

I waited for him to laugh again, but this time he studied me. "Does that mean anything to you?"

"No."

"Not a lesson you've had? A cutout you've used?" he asked, then shook his head in frustration. "A cutout is a go-between two spies might use to carry information between—"

"I know what a cutout is."

"And the pigeons don't mean anything to you?" he asked again.

I closed my eyes, thought back to the feeling of the cold wind on my face and the pressure of Mr. Solomon's hands on my arms, but it was his eyes that I saw most plainly.

"It happened so quickly. He was scared. He wasn't... himself."

"There's good reason for that," the man said without a hint of emotion. "You don't know Joe Solomon."

"You're wrong," I said flatly. "There's been a mistake. Mr. Solomon is on the Gallagher Academy faculty. He's CIA, and he came to London to protect me or warn me or... he was just worried because of the threat."

"You still don't get it, do you?" He was almost smiling as he closed the folder. "Joe Solomon *is* the threat."

"That's ridiculous," I shot back. "Mr. Solomon is my *teacher*."

The man stood. "You can stop calling him 'mister,' young lady." He walked to the door and rapped on the glass. "Joe Solomon will never be your teacher again."

Chapter Six

Over the next six nights the Baxters and I slept in five different safe houses.

There was a seemingly abandoned gardener's shed on an old estate in Scotland, an apartment with a view of Big Ben, a cottage in Wales, and something that could best be described as a small castle, which came complete with a suit of armor and a peacock.

Every morning we would drive. Every second there were guards.

Sure, you might think that having full access to that many covert strongholds would have made Bex and me the envy of the entire student body; but as a rule, we Gallagher Girls don't envy anything that involves guards (when you're the guard*ee*) and spiders (and MI6 safe houses have *a lot* of spiders).

On the sixth night I woke in a narrow bed to the peaceful sound of Bex's breathing and something else—a muffled word: "Cavan."

For a moment, I lay there, then I slipped out of the lower bunk.

The floorboards were surprisingly quiet beneath my bare feet. It was freezing, but I didn't stop to rummage through the duffel bags and suitcases that sat open but neatly packed, ready for a quick escape. Instead, I walked out to the hall and eased toward the narrow, crooked staircase that led from the second story to the small landing outside the kitchen.

Perched on the landing, I could see Mr. Baxter's legs as he sat at the kitchen table, shifting slightly as he spoke. "Have you seen Rachel?"

"Yes," a woman said in a hoarse whisper.

"I'm surprised that was possible," Mrs. Baxter said.

The woman laughed softly. "Well, I wasn't in the mood to hear that it was *impossible.*"

"I see," Mrs. Baxter said.

"Grace, how is she?" the woman asked.

"Fine," Mrs. Baxter said. "Should I go get her?"

"No."

I stood in the dark listening, while the wind blew and the castle moaned and the woman said, "Let the squirt have her sleep."

There was only one person in the world who had ever called me Squirt, so I didn't think—I just stood, ready to bolt down the narrow stairs toward my aunt Abby. But then an arm was around my waist, and a hand clasped over my mouth. I glanced over my shoulder and saw Bex's wide eyes gleaming in the dark.

She shook her head once, quickly. *No,* she was telling me. *Think. We might not get this chance again.*

31

My best friend's smile was especially mischievous (which, believe me, is saying something) as she whispered, "I have a better idea."

Three minutes later I was standing on the top floor of the castle, looking at a small wooden box and a less-than-sturdy rope, listening to my best friend insist, "You should do it."

"Why me?" I whispered, watching as the ancient box dangled in midair over a dark, empty shaft that disappeared into the cold stone of the castle walls.

"You're shorter," Bex said. (Which I am.) "And I'm stronger," she said. (Which she totally might be.) "And I'm..."

"Afraid of spiders?" I guessed.

But Bex plowed on, "...still a little deaf from the percussion grenade incident during finals week."

So, yeah, that's how I ended up in the dumbwaiter.

I felt myself descending through the castle walls, lower and lower, while the noises in the kitchen grew louder and clearer.

"Are you sure you don't want some tea?" Bex's father asked.

"No thanks, Abe." My aunt's voice sounded weak—almost frail. "I haven't been sleeping all that well, to tell you the truth."

"Neither have we," Bex's mother added.

The kettle began to whistle. A chair scraped across the floor.

"How close was it really, Grace?" Aunt Abby asked. "Was she in any danger?"

"Cammie is in constant danger," Mrs. Baxter said as the whistling stopped.

"You saw him, Abe?" Abby asked. Even though there

wasn't a doubt who *he* was, it seemed to take forever for Mr. Baxter to answer.

"Yes."

"How was he?" Abby asked.

"Desperate," Bex's father answered.

"Do you believe it?" Abby asked.

"This is the way the Circle has worked for more than a hundred years...." Mr. Baxter started.

"But, Abe, we *knew* him," Abby pressed again.

After another long pause, Mr. Baxter said, "I believe Joe Solomon is the sort of man that no one will ever truly know."

Three seasoned and decorated operatives sat on the other side of the wall. Between them they'd probably mastered a hundred identities in a dozen countries. Names were just covers. Just legends. Hanging in the darkness, I wondered if anything about Joe Solomon was ever real at all.

It felt as if the truth were slipping away from me, falling, until...

Wait, I realized too late. *I* was slipping—literally.

Through a crack in the top of the dumbwaiter, I could see Bex holding the fraying rope, trying hard to pull me back up, but the rope slipped again.

Outside, the adults kept talking. I heard Mrs. Baxter saying, "We can't tell Cammie until we're absolutely certain...."

"We can *never* tell Cammie," Aunt Abby said.

"Hold on!" Bex's frantic whisper echoed down the shaft as the dumbwaiter dipped again.

This is not good, I told myself. This is not...

But outside the shaft, Mrs. Baxter's voice was calm. "She's almost seventeen, Abby. And the more she knows, the safer she'll—"

"Cammie will never be safe!" Abby said, and I remembered that a semi-stable dumbwaiter was the least of my problems.

"Hang on, Cam," Bex whispered from above. "I'm—"

"We don't know that Cammie would do something foolish," Mrs. Baxter went on.

"Of course she would." Aunt Abby laughed. "*I would*. Trust me, Grace, Abe. Cammie can *never* know—"

Before she could finish, I felt the bottom of the dumbwaiter dropping out from under me as, ten feet up the shaft, the old rope broke and I went hurtling toward the kitchen.

There was a sharp crack as the dumbwaiter reached the base of the shaft, splintering into a million pieces and sending me sprawling onto the kitchen floor.

"What the—" Mr. Baxter started to yell.

With a groan, I rolled over and found myself staring at a pair of gorgeous high-heeled boots, long legs, and a familiar face looking down at me, saying, "Hey, Squirt."

Chapter Seven

"Cammie can never know what?" I asked.

Bex was sitting beside me, the two of us in the hard, straight-backed chairs, looking up at her parents and my Aunt Abby. Bex's hands were rope burned. My elbow was bleeding. But my only concern was what had brought my mother's only sister to England and, most important...

"Cammie can never know what?"

"See?" Abby said, gesturing at the two of us. "This is exactly what I'm talking about."

"It's true." Mr. Baxter crossed his arms and eyed us both. His voice wasn't even a little bit playful as he finished, "They are a liability."

"What can't Cammie know?" Bex asked, choosing, I guess, to let the *liability* thing slide for the time being.

"Go to bed, Cammie," my aunt ordered, sounding exactly like my mother.

"No," I said, sounding exactly like my aunt.

I was pretty sure there was about to be a hole in the time-space continuum, when Abby snapped, "Cameron!"

I was already on my feet. "So you know what *you* would do if you were me, and you knew this big secret..." I leaned across the table, almost daring her as I finished, "Now, imagine what you'd do if there was something you *didn't* know."

As threats go, it was a good one. I could see it in Abby's eyes. After a moment, she pulled out the chair on the other side of the table and sank into it. I tried not to notice the stiffness in the movement or the way she held one arm carefully by her side. I tried not to think about the fact that she'd almost died.

She'd almost died.

She'd almost died.

"We caught one of them." Abby's voice brought me back. "Election night...you were out, and I was..." She trailed off.

She'd almost died.

"From the grab team that came for you, we caught one." My aunt gestured to the place where she'd been shot. "We caught the one who did *this*. A week ago he decided to start talking."

Beside me, I felt Bex shaking, her impatience coming to a boil. "What's this have to do with Mr. Solomon?"

Her father warned, "Rebecca," and Abby carried on.

"The Circle works in cells—small, isolated groups. Two Circle operatives could be sitting right beside each other and not know it. So the man in custody has some knowledge of cell operations, but he doesn't know much. He doesn't even know why they want you, Cammie."

She looked right at me, and I felt my heart fall.

"He only knows the people he's worked directly with and . . ."

As my aunt trailed off, I saw Mrs. Baxter tense. Mr. Baxter brought his hand to his mouth as if he couldn't bear to say the words aloud.

"And he knows the people he was recruited with," Abby said slowly. Her gaze fell to the floor. "When he was at Blackthorne."

For days I'd wanted answers—I'd begged and pleaded for the truth. But now we were there and I didn't want to hear it.

"No. That's just what MI6 thinks, for some reason, but they're wrong. There's been some kind of mistake." I tried to push away, but Abby leaned closer.

"Joe's a double agent, Cam. He was recruited by the Circle a really long time ago."

"How can you say that?" I snapped back. "He's your friend."

"He was also friends with the man who did this!" she yelled, pointing to her injured shoulder. She looked so angry and betrayed, and when she spoke again her voice was more like a plea. "We have to believe it, Cammie. *You* of all people *need* to believe it."

"But . . . he was CIA. . . ." It sounded childish, and yet I had to say it. I was, after all, still a child. "He was our *teacher*. He couldn't have been working for the Circle."

Mrs. Baxter was calm as she took the seat next to Abby. "Think about it, girls. You know having operatives deep inside the Agency would be a high priority for the Circle. And an operative *at* the Gallagher Academy—an operative with so much access to Cammie . . ."

"You're wrong," Bex said.

"It's an old and effective practice," Mrs. Baxter said softly. "Recruit operatives who are young, encourage them to spend their breaks training with the Circle, working with the Circle. And then send them back to school." She was so poised—so good and wise and beautiful that it was almost impossible to doubt her as she looked at us both and said, "But make no mistake, girls. We know what Joe Solomon did over his summer vacation."

"What if he's changed?" Bex challenged. "People change. Maybe he's not working with them anymore."

"It's not the Boy Scouts," Abby answered. "It's not that easy just to walk away."

We sat in silence for a long time before I finally turned back to my Aunt Abby. "Why did you come here tonight?"

"I was worried about you, Squirt. I was—"

"Where's *my mom*?" I heard my voice rising, but I didn't try to stop it.

"She's fine, Squirt." Abby looked at me. "She couldn't come herself, so I came. She's fine."

"*Why* couldn't she come?" I blurted. "What's so important that—"

"All right, then." Mr. Baxter pushed up from the table, signaling that the Q&A portion of our night was officially over. "It's best you two get some sleep. Big day tomorrow. We'll have to get up early to get you back to school."

Tomorrow. School. Bex and I looked at each other. Wordlessly, we both stood and started for the door. Roseville felt a million miles away.

"Abby?" Bex stopped and turned in the doorway, waited for my aunt to look up. "How old . . . When he joined them . . . how old was he?"

Abby's smile was soft but sad. She swallowed hard before she said, "Sixteen."

Chapter eight

How to Return to School
(A list by Cameron Morgan and Rebecca Baxter)

- Do laundry. This is far easier, by the way, when you're at your grandmother's house and not an MI6 safe house (because, while the latter might have far cooler defense mechanisms, the former has a way better laundry room).

- Pack. Which is where living in a series of safe houses comes in handy, because you've never actually *un*packed.

- Set alarms. Because even a Gallagher Girl's internal alarm clock has a tendency to get wonky when you're dealing with vast amounts of stress and jet lag.

- Dress in layers. Because planes are always cold. And also, it's far easier to change your appearance and lose a tail if you can also lose your sweater.

- Double-check that you have the essay you wrote for Culture and Assimilation, the codes you broke for Practical Encryption, and the research paper you did for Covert Operations.

- Take the CoveOps paper out of the bag. Stomp on it. Kick it. Throw it in the trash.

- Take it out of the trash and pack it again. Just in case.

———

It took three planes, two SUVs, and at one point, a very questionable-smelling VW van, but sixteen hours later I found myself staring through bulletproof glass at the bare trees and patches of half-melted snow and ice that lined Highway 10 as it cut through the forest like a snake. After three weeks of living like a gypsy in a foreign land, it felt especially strange to be coming home.

Home.

"Whatcha thinking about, Cam?" Bex poked me and smiled.

"Oh, you know . . . *the usual*," I said as calmly as possible while sitting in the back of a limousine that was as *un*usual as possible. (I'm pretty sure it used to belong to the president.)

"Have you covered vehicular surveillance yet?" Aunt Abby asked.

Bex shook her head.

"Really?" Mrs. Baxter said. She sounded genuinely surprised. "I thought you would have covered that in..."

She trailed off, but I knew what she was going to say: Covert Operations. CoveOps. Mr. Solomon's class.

"Oh well. I guess there's no time like the present." She crossed her legs. "Tell me, Cammie, what do you see?"

"Two cars ahead of us."

"Lead cars, yes." Mrs. Baxter nodded her approval, then turned to her daughter. "Bex?"

"One tail vehicle."

"Right," Mrs. Baxter said. She went on, citing the origins of moving surveillance and protection, something about the chariots of ancient Rome and the death of Caesar, but my mind was drifting. I was watching the dozens of other cars—limousines just like ours (though slightly less bulletproof) that filled the road, waiting to carry my classmates back through our towering gates.

"I've never seen the line so long," Bex said, and I'd been thinking the same thing. "Guards must still be on vacation time," she joked.

Aunt Abby shifted in the seat beside me, but she didn't say anything.

I expected the car to slow and wait its turn in line. But instead, Mrs. Baxter asked, "What's the second rule of countersurveillance?"

"Resist routine and expectations," Bex and I replied just as Mr. Baxter jerked the limo into the passing lane. I felt the car moving faster and faster, flying by the long line of cars waiting to carry my classmates back to school.

Mrs. Baxter sounded just like Bex when she said, "*Exactly.*"

I *know* the Gallagher Academy. I mean, a person doesn't ruin as many white blouses as I have without spending *a lot* of time crawling through filthy sewer lines and secret passageways. So as we flew farther and farther from the gates, I felt pretty certain that we were actually speeding toward . . . nothing. Or so I thought until Mr. Baxter jerked the wheel again and we found ourselves on a narrow lane that, I swear, I'd never seen before.

The good news was that the car was bulletproof and missile proof and had tires that were filled with solid rubber instead of regular air, so they could never, ever go flat.

The bad news was that I was starting to figure out why Bex was such a bad driver, because the rougher the road got, the harder Mr. Baxter pressed on the gas.

"Shortcut," Aunt Abby offered.

"*To where?*" Bex and I both asked.

The car was barreling down the narrow path, tires plunging in and out of rough gorges, mud slamming against the undercarriage. Barren limbs scraped against the sides of the car, and it felt as if we were being swallowed by the forest, driving straight toward an electrified stone wall and at least a dozen of the most highly calibrated security cameras in the world.

"Now?" Mr. Baxter asked from the front seat.

"This'll do," Abby told him.

Mr. Baxter pushed a button on the dashboard and floored the accelerator.

And for the second time during my winter vacation, I saw my (relatively short) life flash before my eyes. I gripped my best friend's hand, waiting for a crash that never came.

Believe it or not, I've never actually been in the Gallagher Academy lake. Well, I hadn't been. Until then.

I still don't know what was most shocking—the feeling of the car hitting some kind of ramp at eighty miles an hour, the sensation of flying through the air and soaring over the fence in a limousine, or the sudden splash that comes when a two-ton car dives nose first into water, seat belts snapping, holding us in place.

I felt the heavy car sinking. Water was over the hood and rising above the windows, but not a drop was seeping inside as we sank below the surface, into the murky darkness of the lake. Fish swam past the windows as if limos drop out of the sky every day—and neither Aunt Abby nor Mrs. Baxter seemed the least bit concerned that our bulletproof car was sinking.

But wait, I realized a second later. We *weren't* sinking.

Bex and I both leaned forward, watched the way the limo's headlights sliced through the water as a propeller emerged from the trunk and began churning, pushing us through the murky haze like a submarine.

"WARNING: RESTRICTED AREA. AUTHORIZED

PERSONNEL ONLY," a shrill mechanical voice ordered in stereo, echoing through the car's speakers.

"Mom..." Bex started, but her mother merely shushed her.

"ACQUIRING RETINAL IMAGES NOW," the voice said just as an orange light flashed through the car like lightning. I squinted, and it felt like a thousand tiny flashbulbs were going off inside my eyes.

"PRESENT VOCAL RECOGNITION, PLEASE," the voice commanded, and my aunt responded, "Abigail Cameron. CIA."

"Abraham Baxter, MI6," Bex's father said from the front seat. Beside me, Bex's mother gave her own name, then nudged me softly in the ribs

"Um...Cameron Ann Morgan...Gallagher Girl?" I didn't have a clue what my official title was or should be. International terrorist target? Teenage girl? Spy in training? Person who really, really wants to know what's going on?

I heard Bex reply in the same way I had, and then the movement stopped. Water fell away as if the car were emerging from the lake, but there was no sunlight streaming through the windows. I peered through the bulletproof glass and saw the headlights sweep over solid stone. Then the car doors popped open automatically, and Abby stepped out, and nothing in my sixteen (almost seventeen!) years of living, or five and a half years of training, had fully prepared me for what I saw.

"There are caves under the lake?" I guessed, but Bex's mother was already out of the car and walking toward the trunk.

I'd heard of underground waterways, caverns, and caves my whole life, but I'd never known I was living right beside one. I stared at the stalactites and stalagmites that covered the cave's floors and ceiling. The ground sloped down behind us, toward the water of the lake while my best friend and I stood on an underground shore, and I remembered that I didn't know all of my school's secrets—not even close.

Before I knew it, Mr. Baxter had our bags out of the trunk and Mrs. Baxter was hugging Bex, whispering in her ear. I was still taking in the long, dark cave that stretched far beyond the headlights' glare.

I stepped to the wall, and ran my fingers along the Gallagher Academy crest that was carved into the stone.

"Good-bye, darling," Mrs. Baxter said. I turned, and she hugged me. Mr. Baxter kissed my cheek. And then Aunt Abby's hands were on my shoulders.

"Cammie, stop for a second. Before you go any farther, I need you to promise me something."

"Okay."

"I need you to be careful this semester." She didn't sound like herself, I realized. She sounded like Mr. Solomon. "Cam, do you hear me?"

"Yes...I know."

"Do not take unnecessary chances."

"I know."

"And, Squirt, you need to be...strong."

I started to tell her again that I knew, but something came over me. "You aren't coming, are you?" I asked.

Abby looked from me to the Baxters and back again. "This is as far as I go."

"But I thought maybe you'd... We won't have a CoveOps teacher."

"Sure you will, Squirt." She smiled slightly. "Sure you will."

Chapter nine

"Dr. Fibs's filing cabinets?" I heard myself mutter five minutes later—still a little shocked, if you want to know the truth. But what else is a girl supposed to feel after riding in an underwater elevator, going through six more scans (two retinal, three voice, and one full-body), and then climbing fifty feet up a rickety staircase that looked older than the school itself?

So, yeah, shock probably covers it. But that didn't stop me from examining the hidden door through which we'd just emerged. "I never knew there was a passageway behind Dr. Fibs's filing cabinets!"

"Which is the sole reason it's still functioning."

Bex and I spun around to see Professor Buckingham behind us, standing in the doorway of the dim room with her arms crossed, looking like the most intimidating barrier of all.

"Cameron, Rebecca, come with me."

There are three things it's important to know about Patricia

Buckingham. 1) She's our oldest faculty member. 2) She is an absolute legend at MI6. And 3) She walks faster than should be humanly possible with a bad hip. At least it seemed that way as Bex and I dragged our heavy bags up the stairs, trying to keep pace.

"I hope your break was nice, ladies." She glanced back at us. "Or as nice as can be expected under the circumstances."

"Professor!" Mr. Mosckowitz called from stairs above us. "I need the—"

"My office. Second shelf," she called back without missing a beat. "I have been asked to convey three very important facts to you both. The first is to remind you that what happened in London is highly classified. Anything you might have seen..." She stopped and stared at us over the top of her glasses. "Any *conversations* you might have had are not to be repeated to anyone—especially your classmates. These are stories you will not share on school grounds."

Bex shot me a quick glance, and knew she'd heard the loophole too. That's probably why Professor Buckingham didn't waste a second before adding, "The second thing is that there will be no more trips off school grounds." She turned to climb again. "Extracurricular or otherwise."

Climbing up the stairs, I watched my teacher turn back to me. "I'm sure we've missed some, Cameron. And if we did... well...I do hope you'll tell us."

Before I could ask exactly *what* they might have missed, I stopped midstride and studied the wall, staring at a piece of molding used to twist and open into a passageway to the barn where we had Protection & Enforcement. The entrance was covered now—a solid wall of stone blocking it forever.

In the first-floor corridor, we passed the place where a grandfather clock used to stand, concealing a trapdoor to the mansion's original ventilation system. . . .

Near the library, I looked for the bookcase that used to swing open to reveal a rope ladder that ran from the mansion's basement to its roof. . . .

But it was gone. They were all gone.

Professor Buckingham must have read my mind, because she stopped at the top of the Grand Staircase and studied me.

"I think, Cameron, that you'll find a lot of things are different."

Armed guards stood in the foyer below us, scanning the fingerprints of my classmates, rifling through their luggage. The stained-glass windows I loved so much were covered with bulletproof glass. The Gallagher mansion had endured hundreds of years of storms and termites and overzealous seventh graders, but in that moment I knew my school was wounded, and all I could do was stand there, staring at its scars.

"They did all this for me?" I wasn't sure how it was supposed to make me feel—flattered or safe or just really, really guilty.

The hallways were quiet. The Hall of History was dark. Below us, the last of our classmates were being cleared to come home, but nothing of the place around me felt like the home I'd left.

Well—that is, until I heard the screaming.

"You're late!"

There was no mistaking Liz's voice. Her accent was stronger, like it always was after a break. And yet as I turned and looked at the incredibly tiny blonde who stood in the mouth of the Hall of History, hands on hips, I was totally *not* expecting what I saw, because Elizabeth Sutton, supergenius and amazing friend, was *angry*.

Not the kind of angry that she gets when she oversleeps and wakes up to study at 6:05 a.m. and not at six sharp—not like how she gets when Bex teases her about her patented study system of color-coded flash cards. Not even the kind of angry that comes with hearing that a teacher won't be offering assignments for extra credit.

Liz was angrier than I'd ever seen her as she looked between the two of us, then threw out her arms. "I have been so worried!" She shot toward us like an eighty-five-pound bullet, grabbing us both, squeezing with more strength than I thought humanly possible (well...when Liz is the human in question). I would have felt pretty lame, except Bex was totally thrown too.

"Hey there, Lizzie," Bex said with what little breath she could draw. "Have a nice holiday?"

But I doubt Liz even heard.

"Why didn't you two call me? Why didn't you e-mail or write or..." She pulled back, then looked from me to Bex. "I told myself that you were probably busy and having fun and... were fine. And then I got back and I saw all the new security measures and I was *so worried!*"

Before I could say a thing, we were back in a dual head-lock, and Liz was breathing deeply. And then, just as quickly, she jerked away.

"So what happened? Where'd you go? What'd you see?"

"Liz, we—"

"I'm afraid that's classified." Buckingham shot me a look as she spoke.

"All of it?" Liz asked.

"All of it," Bex and I answered.

"Patricia!" Mr. Smith was running up the stairs. "We're ready to start the—"

"Coming!" Buckingham called without even a glance. She was too busy looking at me.

"Three things," I told her. "You said there were three things."

"Yes, Cameron, I've been asked to tell you that your mother has been temporarily detained."

"But—"

"She's fine—I can assure you. Just a little delay. But she's not back quite yet."

"Patricia, Harvey seems to think we'll only have one shot at this so..." Our Countries of the World teacher motioned as if to say *let's hurry this along*. And, with that, Professor Buckingham made a move toward the stairs.

"The Welcome Back Dinner will begin shortly," she told us. "You girls go on."

"But..." I started, but then forgot what I was about to say. Because, in the foyer below us, Madame Dabney was helping a senior explain to the guards why she had a fifteenth-century saber in her duffel bag. At the end of the hall, Dr. Fibs was complaining that the entrance to the seventh-grade labs had been moved and he couldn't find it. The Gallagher Academy was stronger than it had ever been—technically. Physically. And yet, in a way, I could almost feel it crumbling around me.

"And, Cameron," Professor Buckingham said from the top of the stairs. "Welcome home."

Climbing the stairs to our room, I tried not to count the secret passageways that we should have passed, but didn't (4); or the underclassmen who suddenly stopped whispering as soon as they saw me (6); or even the number of fingerprint-sensitive doors we had to pass through to reach our suite (9).

I tried to concentrate on how cute Liz's hair looked (because, unlike me, she can totally pull off a bob). I focused on my jetlagged body and my growling stomach (because while MI6 safe houses might be incredibly safe, they do not come particularly well stocked foodwise, let me tell you).

"So I came back a day early to show the formula for my new truth serum to Dr. Fibs," Liz said, eyes shining. "It's ten times more effective than Sodium Pentothal . . . and it makes your teeth whiter . . . and—"

"Wait," I said, stopping in the door to the suite that we'd shared since seventh grade, knowing—sensing—that . . .

"Something's different," Bex said, easing past me into the room.

The beds were made. The curtains were open. Everything

was exactly as it was supposed to be, except . . . it wasn't. There were shoe prints on the freshly vacuumed rug, the faint smell of coffee and strong cologne.

I was stepping toward the dark bathroom, reaching for the light, when Bex yelled, "Wait!"

But it was too late. A strong hand grabbed my wrist. I saw the shadow in the bathroom mirror, looming in the dark. And I didn't hesitate: I stepped back and grabbed the arm that grabbed at me, spinning, using my attacker's own momentum to fling him through the open bathroom door and to the other side of our room.

He smashed into a dresser and sent a lamp crashing to the floor. Then Bex was there, lunging forward with a textbook kick. The man moved quickly, avoiding her foot by inches.

He held out his hands and opened his mouth to speak, but before he could say a word, a Louis Vuitton suitcase came flying into our room, struck the man squarely on his face, and dropped him to the floor like a stone.

"Hey, Macey," I somehow managed to mumble through Bex's hair as my best friend pressed me into the corner of our suite. "That was a nice—"

"Don't move," Macey warned. I wasn't sure if she was talking to me or the man who lay at her feet with blood pouring from his swelling nose. Macey McHenry is one of the most gorgeous girls in the world, but the expression on her face wasn't beautiful in that moment. It was terrifying.

And yet, the man at her feet didn't tremble. Didn't fight.

He just shook his head and said, "Now, I wouldn't do that if I were you."

I followed his gaze to the corner of the room, where Liz was trying to decide whether or not to punch a big red button on the wall marked PANIC BUTTON: TO BE USED IN EMERGENCIES ONLY. I'd never seen it before, but I was fairly certain that pushing it would bring the full force of the Gallagher Academy down upon our suite.

"A strange man is in our room, Liz. Push it!" Bex ordered (sounding a tad irritated that she hadn't been the one to hit him with a suitcase).

"No," I blurted. I looked past the blood and swelling nose and focused on the blue eyes that I'd last seen staring at me across a cold, metal table.

"That's right." The man almost smiled as he stared up the four of us and said, "I'm not a stranger. Am I, Ms. Morgan?"

Chapter ten

So okay, technically I *had* seen him once before, but he was still a total stranger. After all, he hadn't given me his name in London—no rank, no serial number. I knew he had high enough clearance to be in a top secret MI6 facility and an equally top secret school. But if I didn't know Joe Solomon, then I didn't know any man. Especially not that man.

Unfortunately, knowing something and convincing Liz of something are two totally different things.

"But why was *he* doing the security check of our room?" she pleaded after we'd changed into our uniforms and started downstairs. "Is he on the security staff?"

"I'm not sure, Liz," I admitted. "He's just an agent I met in London."

Liz was practically jogging to keep pace beside me, her hand on the banister. "So he was on your protection detail?"

I looked at Bex and shrugged. "Not exactly."

"Did *you* meet him?" Liz asked, whirling on Bex.

"No," Bex said truthfully. "I didn't."

"You left her alone?"

I'd almost forgotten that Macey was there, to tell you the truth. She'd been so quiet, walking ahead of us, but now she was standing at the bottom of the staircase, glaring up at Bex.

"I thought we agreed..." Macey started, then stopped suddenly.

"Agreed to what?" I asked, but got nothing. "What?" I asked again. "Did you guys get together before break and agree to never let me go someplace by myself? Or was it more like an agreement to monitor my mood and behavior so you could warn someone if I was about to crack up and do something stupid?"

My three best friends in the world looked at each other as if they'd all forgotten how to speak English. Finally, Bex said, "Both."

The big double doors of the Grand Hall were standing open. I smelled fresh bread and heard the voices of a hundred girls talking, laughing. I was home. After weeks of running and hiding, I was finally home; but looking at my roommates, I remembered that being a Gallagher Girl isn't about a building. It's about a sisterhood.

I remembered that I'd never really left.

"She didn't leave me, Macey," I said. "They hauled me in for questioning one day, and he's the one who did it." I stepped toward the Grand Hall, with one last smile back at my friends. "She didn't leave me."

* * *

Four things came to mind as I took my regular seat at the junior table. 1) Being on the run in a foreign country is enough to make a girl seriously miss our chef's awesome cooking. 2) The windows of the Grand Hall had been upgraded to a substance that could probably survive a direct hit from a missile. 3) The packets of sweetener on the table now bore the words "The contents of this packet have been certified psychoactive-free."

But it was the fourth thing that I hadn't really been expecting: silence. As soon as I sat down, it felt like the entire table —the entire hall—stopped talking.

Only Bex seemed to be immune to the silence as she threw one long leg over the bench and took her place next to Macey. "Everyone have a good holiday?" She reached for the pitcher of water at the center of the table and filled her glass. And still, the silence drew longer.

"I said," Bex repeated slowly, "*did everyone have a nice holiday?*"

"Yes."

"Sure."

"Uh-huh," everyone hurried to say, but the eyes of my classmates . . . the eyes still stayed on me: Cameron Ann Morgan, Chameleon no more.

And then, just as quickly, their gazes passed to Tina Walters.

"So, um . . . Cammie," Tina started, "how was *your* break?"

"Our holiday was lovely, Tina," Bex answered for me. "Thank you for asking."

Her back was perfectly straight as she said this. She gently shook out a linen napkin and laid it across her lap. Madame Dabney would have been so very proud, but of course Madame Dabney wasn't there—none of our teachers were—so maybe that's why Tina felt safe putting her elbows on the table and leaning closer.

"But did they . . . you know . . . catch them?" she asked, maybe because she's the daughter of both a spy and a gossip columnist and she wasn't going to rest until she heard the full story. Or maybe she was just hoping for a *different* story from the one that should have been obvious to every girl in the (recently reinforced) Grand Hall.

"No, Tina," I said carefully, "they didn't. Not yet."

"But they have a lot of good leads, don't they?" Eva Alvarez asked.

"Of course they do." Bex's gaze found mine, the unspoken words coursing between us: *And his name is Joseph Solomon.*

"Yeah. I bet your mom and Mr. Solomon are going to find something any day now," Anna Fetterman said, and I glanced around the Grand Hall, processing, thinking, realizing that no one had heard a rumor. Not a single one of my classmates had overheard their moms and dads whispering about rogue operatives and sleeper agents in the middle of the night.

"Yeah," Anna said again. "Mr. Solomon will catch them." She nodded and smiled and sounded so sure.

I nodded and smiled and wanted to cry.

To them, Mr. Solomon wasn't a sixteen-year-old boy who had joined the Circle. He was still the man who had walked through the double doors at the back of that very room a year and a half before.

I turned and looked at the doors and almost jumped out of my skin when they swung open—as if I'd willed it to happen, traveled back in time. I half expected to see Joe Solomon among the long line of teachers making their formal entrance down the center aisle. I felt the room around me changing as, one by one, my classmates counted heads, scanned the line, and realized someone was missing.

I was staring down at the table, unable to look, as Tina asked, "Hey, where's Headmistress Morgan?"

Buckingham had said she wasn't back yet. That she was detained ...delayed. And delayed meant running late. Delayed meant "back in a flash."

Buckingham hadn't said *gone*.

"She's got to be here," I said flatly, certain Tina had missed her. "My mom *has* to be back by now," I said, despite the fact that Professor Buckingham was moving to my mother's place behind the podium at the front of the room.

I was standing, desperate for a better look, when Buckingham asked, "Women of the Gallagher Academy, who comes here?" and every girl in the room stood too.

The hall echoed. "We are the sisters of Gillian."

"Why do you come?"

"To learn her skills. Honor her sword. And keep her secrets," my classmates replied, but I didn't say the words. I was too busy staring at Professor Buckingham, who was standing proudly behind the Gallagher Academy crest as if that were her place—her job.

"Welcome back, ladies. I have a few announcements," she said with no more emotion than when we'd stood in the Hall of History and she'd told me my mother had been detained.

"Headmistress Morgan is not able to be with us tonight, so it's my duty to inform you that Joe Solomon will not be teaching our Covert Operations courses this semester."

She said it just like that—no excuses, no explanations—as a gasp went through the room.

"Fortunately, the Gallagher Academy has a long list of alumni and friends from which it can choose its faculty. Therefore, I am pleased to welcome an operative who has excelled on many continents, working in some of the most challenging circumstances that one can experience in the clandestine services."

I knew what she was going to say, of course. A part of me had known it as soon as I had felt the hand on my arm and heard the voice—long before Liz asked her questions. When I turned, I saw those blue eyes staring back at me. I heard Professor Buckingham say, "Please join me in welcoming Agent Edward Townsend."

Watching the man from London make his way down the center aisle, a hundred thoughts rushed through my mind: Who is this guy, really? What does he want with us? Can a suitcase really do that much damage? But Liz was the one who asked what my roommates and I were all thinking.

"We don't like him, do we?"

"No," Bex answered for me as our new CoveOps teacher made his way to the front of the room. "I don't think we do."

He looked directly at me as he passed, but he didn't wink —didn't smile. (Of course, technically, he probably just didn't want to turn his back on Macey.)

"This is probably a good thing, Cam." I could feel Liz staring at me. "The only way your mom and Mr. Solomon would miss the start of school is if they're really close to finding something big. They'll find it and then they'll be back."

"I bet Mr. Solomon is this close to catching the Circle." She looked at me. "Right?"

I know this is going to sound crazy, but when you're a spy, your life isn't defined by the lies you tell, but by the truths. A lie wouldn't change anything. I sat there, numb, knowing that the truth... the truth could set me free.

And that was how I found the strength to whisper, "Mr. Solomon *is* the Circle."

Chapter ELEVEN

In our room an hour later, Bex was the one who told the story. About the Tower and the Circle and the mad look in our teacher's eyes as he stood shaking on the bridge. It sounded like a dozen other crazy tales she'd brought back after break, but this one, I knew, was true.

"He was sixteen?" I watched Liz plug that number into some formula in her mind, then shake her head as if it didn't compute. "No, he couldn't have been bad. I mean he *can't* be. He is...I mean, he was..."

"Our age," Macey finished for her.

One of the downsides of going to a school where they teach you that you're capable of anything is that eventually you start to believe it. But none of us had ever thought ourselves capable of that.

"How does someone our age end up working for the Circle?" Macey asked in disbelief.

"Blackthorne," I said simply. "The Circle recruits at Blackthorne."

"Cammie, no," Liz started, already knowing where my thoughts had gone. "Zach can't be . . ."

"But he *might* be. These are the facts: We know the Circle recruits at Blackthorne. We know Zach was in London. And D.C. And Boston. Zach knew the Circle wanted me before *we* even knew the Circle existed." I looked down at my hands. "And we know Zach's always been close to Mr. Solomon. They've both always known too much."

"Cam, no," Macey ordered. "Stop it. Even if Mr. Solomon is a double agent or whatever, that doesn't mean Zach is too."

"Bex's mom said that having someone at the Gallagher Academy—having someone close to me—would be a high priority." I laughed sadly. "And Zach got pretty close."

"Cam, that doesn't mean anything." Liz rushed toward me. "Maybe Mr. Solomon used to work for the Circle, but now—"

"He's the good guy?" I guessed.

"Yeah," Liz said.

"Good guys don't jump into rivers in the middle of winter to get away from the other good guys," I answered. "Besides, I don't think the Circle really offers early retirement."

"Okay, so Joe Solomon's a traitor. . . ." Macey said as simply as if she'd said "So Joe Solomon looks good in turtlenecks." "Do you really think he'd be *stupid*, too?" She stepped closer. "Think about it, Cammie. Why was Mr. Solomon there?"

"He said I had to follow the pigeons."

"Follow the what?" Liz asked.

"He was talking crazy, okay?" I took a deep breath. "One second he was telling me to run, and then... you know."

"So you're saying that one of the CIA's best undercover operatives—not to mention one of the most wanted men in the world—walked through an MI6 surveillance detail just to tell you to follow the pigeons?" Macey didn't try to hide her disbelief.

"Yeah," I said. "He said he had to see me before I got back to school. And he said when I got back to school I had to *follow the pigeons*."

"Tell me this, Cam." Macey placed her arm around my shoulder. She seemed so much taller than me then. "Do you believe Mr. Solomon is working for the Circle?"

"Abby and the Baxters say he is."

"What do *you* say?" Macey asked.

"It's true," Bex answered for me, leaning against the wall, arms crossed. "My mum and dad have been taking me on missions since before I could walk. They've never lied to me before. They wouldn't start lying to me about this." She turned and looked right at me. "Abby would never lie to *you* about this."

Sometimes I hate it when my friends are right. Unfortunately, it happens *a lot*.

"But, Bex, your parents weren't there on election night," Macey countered. "Abby was there, but she was half dead. Cam, you were drugged and practically knocked unconscious, so you won't remember either—but I do." She shivered a little.

"I remember everything. Everyone was worried that night, but Mr. Solomon was terrified. He was as worried about you as your mother was."

"Mr. Solomon's been working for the Circle since he was sixteen! He's pretty good at faking things," Bex challenged.

Macey shook her head. "He wasn't faking."

"You can't know that," Bex said.

Macey laughed softly. "I know fake love when I see it."

I didn't know what so say, so I sank to the floor and rested my arms on my knees, suddenly far too tired for the first day of school.

On the other side of the room, Liz sat perfectly still on her bed, weighing options, waiting to cast the tie-breaking vote. When she spoke, her voice was low. "Cam, where's your mom?"

"Buckingham said she's been temporarily detained. Whatever that means." I sighed. "She didn't even come to England after . . . everything."

"I wish she was here," Bex admitted. "There is something they're not telling us."

I pictured Zach, his breath fogging in the air as he'd said *They know more than we know.* But my mother was gone. The Baxters and Abby were a thousand miles away. That morning Bex and I had walked away from England—from our last chance at answers—except . . .

I smiled.

"Cam," Liz said softly. "What is it?"

"Townsend."

"What?" Liz said. "Do you think he's going to be a good teacher?"

I shook my head.

"Do you think he's hot?" Macey asked.

I laughed.

"Then *why* are you smiling?" Liz's voice went up an entire octave, but I just looked at her—thought about a folder on a metal table and eyes that looked like they'd seen everything.

"I think he *knows things.*"

Chapter twelve

Covert Operations Report

When Operatives Morgan, McHenry, Baxter, and Sutton (hereafter referred to as The Operatives) returned to the Gallagher Academy for the spring semester of their junior year, they were faced with an absent mother-slash-headmistress, a fugitive former teacher, and a tall, dark, and cocky new faculty member who, presumably, knew far more than he was saying.

The Operatives were resolved to make him <u>say</u>.

The first day of the semester started as semesters often do.

Mr. Smith gave a really good pop quiz on the world's most unstable political regimes and the top five ways to undermine each. By midmorning Madame Dabney was passing out place cards and instructing us all to prepare a seating chart for a state dinner that includes two ambassadors, five senators, and three rogue operatives who may be selling nuclear technology to the highest bidder.

But walking out of Madame Dabney's tearoom that Monday morning, I couldn't help but remember that nothing would ever be "typical" again.

"That's it. It's official!" Tina Walters whispered to me. "Joe Solomon is in deep."

I shot an anxious glance at Bex, but Tina went on slowly, savoring every word.

"According to my sources, he hasn't been farmed out to any cooperating agencies. He's not listed on the in-action list. And he's not exactly the type for *official* cover operations, so wherever he is . . . our teacher is in deep, deep cover."

The entire junior class seemed to exhale, and I recognized the look that was spreading through the narrow hall. If possible, Joe Solomon had just gotten cooler. And hotter.

"I bet he and your mom are on some super-secret and dangerous mission, Cam," Courtney Bauer guessed as we emerged into the main corridor on the second floor.

"*Yeah.*" Anna Fetterman's voice had taken on a dreamy quality. "I bet your mom and Mr. Solomon are going to find them. I bet . . ."

Anna went on, but I tuned out, barely registering the sounds of my school—slamming doors and running girls. I looked into the center of the foyer below, where a half dozen teachers stood huddled together in a way I'd never seen before.

"Cam?" Anna asked. "Are you okay?"

One by one the teachers in the foyer began to break away and start down the halls or up the stairs.

"Cam?" Anna asked, her voice higher.

"Sorry, Anna," I muttered. "I've . . . got to go."

Professor Buckingham was already at the top of the Grand Staircase, walking toward the Hall of History, when I cried, "Professor? Professor Buckingham!"

"Yes, Cameron?" She didn't snap the words, but they sounded weary. She seemed tired as she stood beside the sword that had belonged to Ioseph Cavan. "Is there something I can help you with?"

I wanted to know why my mother's door was closed to everyone, even me. I wanted to ask how it could be true about Mr. Solomon—how it could be true at all. But there was only one thing that I knew it was okay to ask.

"It's spring," I said.

"It is?" Professor Buckingham glanced out a window streaked with freezing rain.

"I mean, it's the spring semester. You said last fall that you might be able to teach me about the Circle of Cavan in the spring. And . . . it's spring."

All around us, girls were filing into classrooms, rushing out the front doors to P&E. The halls were growing quiet. School was back in session—life was back to normal. But behind Patricia Buckingham, my mother's office door stayed closed.

"Junior year curriculum is very challenging, Cameron dear," she said.

"I know, that's why I—"

"You need to focus and learn as much as you can."

"I know, but the Circle is—"

"Cameron, the lessons of this school are essential for fighting the evils of the world—no matter what that evil calls itself. *You have to learn those lessons,*" she snapped, and I knew it wasn't advice; it was an order. And she was right. My classes weren't less important now. Not by a long shot.

"And even if that were not the case, I'm afraid there are a number of . . . *pressing* matters that require my attention for the time being."

And then it hit me: for the first time that I could remember, our oldest faculty member looked . . . old.

Her hands were dry. Her eyes were puffy. And I could have sworn I heard her voice crack as she said, "Now, if I'm not mistaken, you're about to be late for Covert Operations. You don't want to keep our newest teacher waiting."

Chapter Thirteen

Running through the halls toward the elevator to Sublevel Two, I tried to brace myself for what I had to do.

1. Learn what (if anything) Agent Townsend knew about my mother, Mr. Solomon, and the Circle of Cavan.

2. Discern whether Agent Townsend would lean toward practical or theoretical examinations and how to best master each. (Because being the target of an international terrorist organization is no excuse for letting your GPA slide.)

When I reached the small hallway beneath the Grand Staircase and the large mirror that was supposed to slide aside and show me the way to the Covert Operations classrooms, I pressed my hand against it and waited for the eyes of the painting behind me to flash green. But the glass beneath my palm stayed cool, and nothing happened.

It was my first lecture with Agent Townsend, and I was *already* late. I actually knocked on the mirror as if there were someone back there, waiting to let me in.

Still nothing.

I was turning, starting for one of the other elevators, when I saw it: a small, neatly typed piece of paper taped to the wall.

ATTENTION STUDENTS: UNTIL FURTHER NOTICE, THE SUB-LEVELS WILL BE CLOSED. ALL COVERT OPERATIONS COURSES WILL TAKE PLACE IN ROOM 132.

I didn't know what was happening. All I knew for certain was that I was late, so I turned on my heel and ran through the empty hall, past the library and the student lounge—all the way to the classroom that had been nothing but a big storage closet at the end of last semester. I almost ran right past it, but at the last second I grabbed the door frame and skidded to a stop.

"Oh, there you are."

Okay, I don't know about regular schools, but let's just say that at the world's premiere spy school, tardiness isn't exactly *typical*. And when it does happen, it's almost always met with questions like "Was there an explosion in the chemistry lab?" or "Do you have another concussion?" It is most certainly *never* met with "Oh, there you are."

But those were the words Agent Townsend chose, and for someone who had questioned me in a top secret facility just hours after one of the world's most wanted men had pseudo-kidnapped me, he certainly didn't seem that concerned with where I'd been.

"I'm sorry, I—"

"Just . . . sit," he said with barely a glance in my direction.

I took the desk next to Bex, and without looking at the clock, I knew I was three and a half minutes late. Three and a half minutes in which my classmates had been sitting in silence, waiting. And as I joined them, I realized our teacher *wasn't* waiting for me.

Four minutes.

Five minutes.

Ten minutes, we waited. The only noise was the sound of Agent Townsend turning the pages of his newspaper.

It was a test, I told myself. He wanted to see if we were memorizing the front page of the paper he held; he was gauging how still we could be, how silently we could sit. Great operatives are naturally patient, I thought. He wanted to see if we could wait.

Little did he know, Tina Walters doesn't wait for anyone. (Or, well, she does, but evidently she draws the line at ten minutes.)

"Mr. Townsend?"

Our teacher didn't glance up, didn't say a single word.

"Sir," Tina went on, "is there something we could do to help you get started with your lecture?" She sounded very much like Madame Dabney, but Mr. Townsend wasn't impressed.

"No," he said flatly, then raised his newspaper higher, threw his feet to the desktop, and leaned back in his chair. "Who can tell me about Joe Solomon?"

It sounded like a pop quiz. It *looked* like a pop quiz. But I couldn't shake the feeling that the entire junior class had just been picked up and hauled across the Atlantic—plopped down inside Baring Cross Station.

Townsend moved the paper aside for a split second and pointed to Tina Walters, who was about to pull her arm out of its socket, she was raising her hand so wildly. "You," he said.

"Agent Joseph Solomon. CIA operative. Faculty member of the Gallagher Academy for Exceptional Young Women—"

"Know all that," our new teacher interrupted. "Next."

"He said that after break we would probably start with secret writing techniques," Anna told him. "And if that went well, he promised we could—"

"Boring," Townsend countered.

I could feel my classmates watching closer, sitting up straighter—literally rising to the challenge. But I knew this was no test—it was an interrogation. We weren't students in that moment; we were witnesses who'd been locked in a room with a double agent almost every day for a year and a half.

"Where did he go?" Agent Townsend slowly turned the page of his paper. "How did he fill his days? What did he want ...here?"

"He's a teacher," Eva Alvarez said. "He wanted to teach."

Agent Townsend laughed, quickly and softly, but there was no joy in his voice as he said, "I'm sure he did."

"I'm sorry, sir?" Anna said. "I don't understand."

"I'm sure you don't," he muttered.

The Operatives were able to ascertain that whatever brought Agent Townsend to the Gallagher Academy, it was NOT a love of teaching.

Then the feet came off the desk and the paper went down and I got a good look at his swollen nose (note to self: even soft-sided luggage can make an excellent weapon).

"*Where* does he spend his time?"

"Well, usually we see him in Sublevel Two," Tina admitted, and an odd look crossed Agent Townsend's face.

"Nowhere else?"

"Everywhere else," Anna replied.

It occurred to me then that it would have been a good lesson—a test of our memories, of our powers of observation. But Agent Townsend didn't know that. Agent Townsend didn't care.

"Known associates?" he asked, then shook his head as if for a second he'd forgotten that he thought we were idiots. "I mean, who were his friends? Did he have any allies? Anyone he was especially close to?"

"Sometimes he lets Mr. Mosckowitz go with us on missions," Anna said.

"He used to work out in the P&E barn with Mr. Smith," Kim Lee added.

"I think he might be *really* close to Headmistress Morgan." Tina giggled, but then glanced at me and stopped.

"Is that so?" Townsend crossed his arms and looked at me. "What about you, Ms. Morgan? What do you know about Joseph Solomon?"

Freezing rain hit against the windows. I shivered, remembering the cold wind and the look in Mr. Solomon's eyes as we stood on the bridge, and the fact that I'd believed him. For a year and a half, I'd believed everything.

The Operatives hated Joe Solomon.

"Sir." I heard Bex's voice. "Mr. Solomon used to say that an operative's best weapon is her memory, and that—"

Agent Townsend finally stopped staring at me. "You're the Baxter."

"Yes, sir." Bex beamed.

"I know your parents' work," he said.

Bex smiled. "Thank you, sir."

"That wasn't a compliment."

The Operatives missed Joe Solomon.

Townsend stood and walked around his desk, settled back in his chair. "I've known about the Gallagher Academy and its girls for most of my career." He leveled us with a gaze. "And that wasn't a compliment either."

I noticed something about his accent then. I replayed his words in my mind while, outside, the sleet fell harder, and the room turned colder, and I knew the entire class was starting to feel the chill.

"Fine, if this is all any of you are willing to bring to today's—"

"How long were you stationed in Mozambique?"

Townsend was rarely surprised, I could tell, and yet my question stopped him. "Excuse me?" he said.

"Your Swahili this morning at breakfast was very distinctive." He looked at me as if he wanted to protest, but I didn't give him the chance. "You're left-handed, but the calluses on your palm say that you probably shoot with your right hand." I thought of how he'd moved when he pulled his feet from the desk. "You favor your left knee. I'm betting you hurt it . . . what? Six months ago. Your accent is lower middle-class, but you went to a good school, didn't you? Someplace like this, I'm betting."

"Nice trick, Ms. Morgan."

"It's not a trick." I shook my head. "It's last fall's midterm. Mr. Solomon—"

"Joe Solomon is gone," he snapped. "I made that point very clearly in London, or have you forgotten?"

I'd forgotten nothing about that day—not the color of Townsend's shirt or the cool feel of the hard, metal table.

"Why aren't we having this class in Sublevel Two?" I asked, and watched his eyes change. "Were you not given clearance?"

"Oh, I assure you, Ms. Morgan, I'll see all of this school I need to see." He waved toward the door. "Now go. Consider yourselves dismissed."

Chapter fourteen

Over the course of the following week, The Operatives were able to ascertain the following:

- The word "pigeon" appeared in none of Joseph Solomon's case files, legend histories, or lesson plans.
- There are approximately 4,902 Pigeon Roads, Pigeon Lanes, Pigeon Rivers, etc. in the United States—not one of which was in Roseville, Virginia.
- An incredibly thorough search of the Gallagher Academy servers revealed no secret database labeled "Mr. Solomon's Super-Secret Pigeons File," as much as The Operatives wanted to find one.
- As far as mysteries go, "the pigeons" had nothing on Agent Townsend.

* * *

"This is useless," Liz exclaimed, her voice echoing off the high-vaulted ceiling of the P&E barn.

"No it's not," Bex said, grabbing the crossbow out of her hand. (Oh yeah, I said *crossbow*.) "All Gallagher Girls have to be proficient with two weapons, and I'm telling you the crossbow is—"

"Not *this*," Liz said, grabbing the weapon back and giving it a good shake (at which point both Macey and I dropped to the floor and took cover). "*Operation Townsend*," she whispered.

Outside, a fresh blanket of snow was falling over the grounds, and the tall windows were covered with fog. Sophomores fenced on the mats below us. A group of seventh graders were braving the climbing wall, while the whole barn echoed with the thuds and cries of girls who had been locked inside for way too long.

"The man is a ghost, guys," Liz said, her voice low. "I mean, seriously ghosty. He went to some ritzy boarding school in England on scholarship—"

"Good call on that, by the way," Bex told me, but Liz never even slowed down.

"Then he joined MI6 right out of college. I'm pretty sure he was stationed in eastern Europe, because he did that big sting operation in Romania ten years ago."

"The one with the vampire bats?" Bex asked, eyes wide.

"Yeah," Liz said, eyes wider. "And I'm pretty sure he was the one who took down that group of KGB generals who were smuggling old Soviet missiles using a traveling circus as cover."

"Operation Big Top?" Bex exclaimed.

"Uh-huh," Liz said. "But then...after that...it's like he disappeared. I mean...nothing."

"Which means something," I said, and Liz nodded slowly.

"Something big."

"Bex, what does our surveillance tell us?" I asked, turning to the girl beside me.

"He never takes the same route twice; barely eats, barely sleeps, and confides in absolutely no one."

"He's up to something," I said. "This guy doesn't do anything by accident, so if he's here, it's for something big, and it doesn't have anything to do with teaching."

"Liz," Macey said, panic in her voice. "Liz, you're going to want to hold that—"

"Sorry!" Liz yelled to the girls on the rock wall, who now had to navigate around an arrow.

"Hey, Morgan!"

I turned and saw Erin Dillard walking through the barn, as if members of the senior class regularly came up to talk to juniors, which, let me tell you, they don't. "We need to talk."

"Hi, Erin," I said. "Did you have a nice winter—"

"Where's your mother?" As soon as Erin spoke, I knew this wasn't a chat. It was a mission.

"I'm not sure."

"Do you know how to get a message to her?" Erin asked. "Dead letter drop? Cutout? Anything?"

"What's wrong?" I asked.

"What do you think? Townsend. I'm a senior, Morgan," Erin said with a cautious look around the barn. "I got offered a spot in the MI6/CIA Cross-Agency Deep Cover Training Program."

"That's awesome," Bex said, but Erin merely shrugged.

"Thanks. I got the letter over break. I'm supposed to report to work—*to work*—in June, and do you know what our Cove-Ops homework was this weekend?"

We all shook our heads.

"We didn't have any."

"No!" Liz exclaimed.

Erin nodded. "A few months from now I'm going to be in deep cover somewhere, and *this* is how I'm supposed to get ready?"

She was right, of course. Mr. Townsend's class wasn't just a waste of time. It was dangerous.

Erin shook her head, then turned to stare out the window and together we watched our newest teacher walk across the grounds then disappear without a trace into the falling snow. "What's he *really* doing here?"

Erin's a great student. She's going to be an awesome spy. As she turned and walked away, her whisper seemed to echo, settling down on the four of us. Our mission was clear.

"He'll be a hard target," Bex said.

"I know."

"We're talking this-guy-makes-Mr.-Smith-look-like-a-candy-striper hard."

I nodded. "Yeah. That's right."

"So the question is," Bex said slowly, "how far are you willing to go?"

I looked at my three best friends in the world. "How far is there?"

Chapter fifteen

Covert Operations Report

Operatives Morgan, Baxter, Sutton, and McHenry began a dangerous information-seeking operation on a highly hostile target. And teacher.

The Operatives were able to ascertain the following:

- Agent Townsend never sleeps past eight or goes to bed before two.
- The Target runs five miles every day and was seen doing 500 sit-ups in a row (which, according to Operative Baxter, isn't nearly as impressive as it sounds).
- The Target strictly avoids both sugar and caffeine (which, according to Operative Morgan, is every bit as crazy as THAT sounds).

- Despite two weeks on the Gallagher Academy faculty, The Target has acquired zero friends.

I've had a lot of memorable meals in five and a half years at the Gallagher Academy, but that was one of the few times when I didn't actually *eat* anything.

"He's not coming," Liz said, her gaze glued to the big double doors at the back of the room. Bex and Macey and I stayed quiet, glancing around the Grand Hall, the two of them picking at their food as we took turns staring at the doors.

Liz was the one who voiced what we were all thinking. "What if he doesn't come?"

"Hey, Macey, can I have that—"

"No!" the four of us cried in unison. Macey grabbed a banana out of Courtney Bauer's hands, which might have looked kinda strange. And, okay, so maybe the fact that, between the four of us, we'd taken one of everything on the buffet *was* kinda strange. But at the Gallagher Academy, "strange" is a completely relative thing.

"Sorry, Courtney," I said, trying to explain. "It's just that we've got this experiment we're going to do later with . . ."

But then I couldn't finish because Agent Townsend was standing at the entrance of the Grand Hall, taking a long drink from a bottle of water. His dark curly hair was wet with sweat. In his black running suit, he looked as if he could have just gotten back from breaking into an embassy, parachuting behind enemy lines, meeting with a particularly shady informant in the darkest alley of the most dangerous city in the world. As much as I wanted to hate Agent Townsend, there was one thing I didn't dare forget: he was probably a very good spy.

I looked at my roommates, knowing that for the next hour, somehow, someway, the four of us had to be better.

"Who has eyes?" I whispered as I felt the man pass behind me.

"He's going to the buffet," Bex said, but unless you could hear her you would have sworn she was talking about the weather.

"What's he doing?" Liz asked. (Her face and voice, I'm sorry to say, were significantly less covert.)

"Apple," Macey said. Her blue eyes seemed especially big and bright as she looked at me and whispered again, "Apple."

It took four seconds for Liz to take the syringe from her bag. Her hands were shaking as I pulled the apple from my tray and held it beneath the table.

"You do realize this is probably illegal, right?" I asked, but Liz looked up at me and smiled as if I were the most naïve girl in the world.

"It can't be illegal, Cam. It's *research*."

So that was it. Our teacher's fate, my safety, and Liz's GPA all hinged on what we were about to do.

"You're doing great, Lizzie," Bex said, but still Liz's hand trembled.

"Liz . . ." Macey started.

"Got it!" Liz said, and in the next second the apple passed beneath the table from Liz's hand to Bex's.

In a flash, Bex was up and walking toward the door while Townsend did the same. Three seconds later my best friend was stumbling into him. The apple he'd been carrying slipped from his grasp and tumbled through the air, right into Bex's outstretched palm.

"Mind where you're going, Baxter," he said as she handed one apple back to him. But there was a glint in Bex's eyes as she turned her back to us, pulled another apple from behind her back, and took a big bite.

I just sat there wondering what Grandma Morgan would say if she knew what we were doing—no doubt something about forbidden fruit.

The Operatives engaged in a basic four-man rotating surveillance detail, tracking The Target through the Gallagher Mansion.

It would have been nice to have had comms units. Every operative in the world can tell you the extreme disadvantages of tailing someone who knows what you look like. And to be perfectly honest, it's always easier when your co-agents are all well-trained and confident field agents and not . . . well . . . Liz.

"Oopsy daisy," Liz whispered as she missed a step on the big stone staircase that led to the old chapel.

I could hear Townsend's steps in the corridor above me. After forty-five minutes of following him through the library and watching from a window while Bex trailed him across the grounds—not to mention one very scary moment involving Liz, a suit of armor, and Professor Buckingham's black cat—my roommates and I paused on the steps, listening as Townsend walked faster, but toward what or who, I didn't know until I heard him call, "Mosckowitz, a word."

"Oh, hello, Agent Townsend! Out for a run, I see. I tried running for a while. It wasn't really a good...fit for me."

Which was sort of an understatement if you ask any of the girls who remember the semester we had to have encryption lessons on the ground floor because Mr. Mosckowitz sprained both his ankles by falling into a ditch.

I watched Bex ease ahead, then signal to the three of us to follow her up the stairs. Crouched on the landing, I could see two shadows—Agent Townsend's much longer and leaner than Mr. M.'s—as they stretched across the floor.

"Look here, Mosckowitz," Townsend said. I didn't hear a footstep but I saw his shadow move. "I was told you were a codes man."

"I...I am," Mr. Mosckowitz said, but he sounded like he didn't quite believe it.

"I was under the impression that you were the best."

"I'm...pretty good," Mr. Mosckowitz said, which was perhaps the understatement of the century.

"So why haven't you cleared up this mess with the sublevels? They're used for the instruction of Covert Operations, are they not?" Townsend said.

"Well, yes..."

"And I am the Covert Operations instructor, am I not?"

"Someone needs to instruct *him*," Bex whispered, but my best friend didn't move. We all stayed silent, staring at the two shadows on the floor.

"Well, see, it's . . . complicated," Mr. Mosckowitz said.

"*Un*complicate it," said Townsend.

"Every generation adds a new level of defenses, and while the new ones are . . . well, they're *good*, the old ones are . . ."

"What?" Townsend snapped.

"Old," Mr. Mosckowitz said simply. "Dr. Fibs and I have been working on a theory about how some of the older mechanisms might work, but to tell you the truth, most of them weren't meant to be overridden. If they were ever activated, it was supposed to be . . ." He made a gesture with his hands. "Ka boom."

Townsend gave a slow laugh. "And you and Buckingham wouldn't be slow-playing this process, would you?"

"We could override the more recent safety protocols, and you could go down there tonight, but . . ."

"What?"

"Some of the most top secret artifacts in the world might be destroyed, and . . ."

"What?"

"You'd probably die." Mr. Mosckowitz's shadow moved across the floor, easing away.

And then the longer shadow tossed something high into the air. I saw it tumbling, spinning. The hand that reached out to catch it moved as fast as light.

"I want access to those sublevels, Mosckowitz." There was a sickening crunch as Townsend took a bite. "Make it happen. Make it happen soon."

"Liz!" Bex hissed twenty minutes later. "How much did you put in there?"

Liz shrugged and looked slightly guilty. And slightly wicked. It was a terribly evil combination. "I couldn't be sure he'd eat it all, and if he just took one bite, that might not be enough to—"

"Liz," I whispered, needing her to get to the point.

"Five times more than recommended!" she blurted.

At the end of the hall I heard a crash. Our four heads peered around the corner just in time to see Agent Townsend stumble away from the shards of a shattered vase.

We looked at Liz, who whispered, "Maybe six."

When we turned back to the hall, Townsend was standing thirty feet away, staring at us. I was sure we were busted. But then Agent Townsend stopped and gave a sloppy wave.

"I'm going to my room!" he called, and then he turned and collapsed onto the plush cushions of one of my favorite window seats. He tried to pull the red velvet curtains around him like a blanket.

"What are you doing in my room?" he snapped as I appeared beside him. And then he seemed to realize that his "room" was two feet deep and three feet long. "Is this my room?"

I shook my head. "No."

"Oh." His blue eyes had warmed somehow, as though something in that apple had caused all of his defenses to thaw.

"Should we ask him something to . . . you know . . . test it?" Macey asked.

When my roommates looked at me, I realized we hadn't had interrogation training yet. Not even Mr. Solomon had taught us how to do this.

Fortunately, as with most things covert, Bex was a natural.

"Is there really a Loch Ness Monster?" she asked.

Townsend shrugged. "Of course there is. Chemical warfare training went awry in the thirties. Had to lock the thing up somewhere."

"Were the crown jewels really stolen and replaced with fakes in 1962?"

He smiled. "Only the rubies."

"Where is Mr. Solomon?"

"That, I do not know." He raised his eyebrows. "Yet."

"Why are the CIA and MI6 after Mr. Solomon?"

"Oh, you know that, Ms. Morgan." Despite the slurred speech, the words were enough to make my heart race. "Anyone who has been a part of the Circle since the age of sixteen is someone we would like to have a chat with."

"Why did you come here?" Bex asked.

"To track a fox, you start at its den."

"What do you know about my mother?"

Townsend turned his head toward the window. His breath fogged up the glass. I was beginning to think he hadn't heard me when he whispered, "They won't hurt her."

And with those words, a dread like I had never known filled my chest. "Someone has my mother?" I grabbed his shirt and pulled him closer, forced him to look at me. "Who?" I shook him. "Who has her?"

His smile was oddly vacant. *"We do."*

My hands went rigid, forming fists around his collar.

"We? Who's 'we'? *Where is my mother?*" I yelled, but Townsend was drifting. His eyelids fluttered. He stared out the wavy glass as if he'd never seen a window before.

"It *is* beautiful here," he said, then closed his eyes and drifted off to sleep.

I released my grasp, watched him land against the pillows. He looked as peaceful as a baby.

And then Liz slapped him. Yes, actual slappage.

He shuddered awake, his eyes clear for one brief second.

"No!" Liz yelled, slapping him again. "You're wrong!" she snapped.

"Liz . . ." Bex reached for her, but Liz lashed out again.

"You're wrong!" she yelled. "Mrs. Morgan is going to come back, and we're going to clear Mr. Solomon's name, and then this school will have a real teacher again."

"Oh now, I doubt that." There was something of the man from London creeping back into his voice. He smiled. "I don't think Rachel Morgan would want to work beside the man who killed her husband."

Chapter Sixteen

It was too hot inside the mansion. I remember passing roaring fires and foggy windows—pushing through crowded hallways as if I might never breathe fresh air again. Fire. It felt like the world was on fire.

"Cammie!" Bex called behind me, but I didn't stop until I was across the foyer and pushing against the heavy doors.

I didn't have a coat. The sky above me was heavy, dark, and gray as I crossed the field that stretched from the mansion to the woods.

"Cammie," Bex called again. Behind her, I saw Liz and Macey running closer.

"Cam, are you okay?" Liz called, and I whirled.

"No!" I didn't know I was shouting. I only knew the word had been trapped inside of me, boiling. "No! I'm *not* okay."

My roommates stopped, frozen. They seemed afraid to get too close.

"We don't know what he meant by that," Liz told me. "We don't know where he got his information or if his sources are secure. We don't know what that meant."

"No." I shook my head. "That's just it. We don't know *anything*. I know bombs and antidotes and how to say 'parakeet' in Portuguese, but I don't know where my father is buried."

Liz's eyes were red as they stared into mine. "Cammie, it's okay. It's going to be okay."

"Mr. Solomon killed my dad. Mr. Solomon..."

As I trailed off, Bex stepped closer. She reached for me, but I jerked away.

"They want me...alive." Hot tears stung inside my eyes. My throat burned. "They *need* me alive!" I screamed, unable to stop the words. "How am I supposed to be? What am I supposed to feel?"

"I know how you feel, Cam," Macey said.

"You don't—"

"Cammie!" I'll never forget the tone of Macey's voice in that moment. "Cam," she said slowly, moving toward me, "I know how it feels to be watched every second of every day. I know what it's like to trust fewer and fewer people until it seems like you are completely alone in the world. I know you think that the only things that are left in your life are the bad things. I know what you're feeling, Cam." Her hands were on my shoulders. Her blue eyes were staring into mine. "*I know.*"

For two months I'd lived with the knowledge that the Circle of Cavan was after me, thinking that no one could possibly know what that felt like. Like no matter where you were or who you were with, you were never safe. But I was wrong . . . someone did. And she was standing right in front of me.

"He won't tell me where my mother is," I said softly. "Agent Townsend knows—he knows! And he won't—"

"We'll find her, Cam," Bex said, reaching for me. "We will."

"Yeah," Liz said, joining us.

"We'll track your mom down—track her to the end of the earth if we have to—and then we'll ask her . . ."

The air felt warmer with my friends there around me. I felt my heartbeat start to slow as I heard a voice behind me say, "Ask me what?"

Chapter Seventeen

She was there. My mother was there. It felt so strange to see her—to hear her voice, watch the way she walked with us through the front doors and up the Grand Staircase—as if nothing at all had happened since putting me in a limo with the Baxters in December and waving good-bye.

"Mom, I—"

"It's good to see you, kiddo." She put her arm around me and held me tightly as we reached the Hall of History. "Did you and Bex have a nice break?"

She hadn't called on Christmas morning. She hadn't come to London after what happened on the bridge. She had been absent from our school for almost a month, and yet as I watched her unlock her office door, there was only one question I wanted answered.

"Is it true?"

The Baxters and Aunt Abby and even Agent Townsend

had told me the facts, but only my mom could make me believe them. "Is Mr. Solomon really part of the Circle?"

I heard chatter coming from the halls, but my classmates felt a million miles away as my mother stepped into the dark room and softly whispered, "Yes."

She started toward her desk. Inside her office, I felt brave enough to ask, "Did he kill Dad?"

"The Circle has a long history of recruiting agents very young, Cammie. When Mr. Solomon joined, he would have been—"

"*Did he kill my father?*"

"Cammie, sweetheart..."

My lips began to tremble. The pressure I'd been feeling for months rose and swelled, and then I couldn't stop it. The world was blurry and my cheeks were wet, and no matter how hard I tried, it was like I'd forgotten how to breathe.

"I'm so sorry, Cammie. I'm so sorry."

"Where were you?" I could hear my voice breaking. "I *needed* you."

"Cam," my mother said softly. "I knew you were safe, sweetheart. The Baxters are good people—they're great operatives—"

"They aren't my family. I needed *you!*"

"Sweetheart, believe me, I wanted to come to you, but it wasn't possible."

I wanted to believe her, but Agent Townsend was like a ghost, whispering in my ear: *They won't hurt her.*

"Why didn't you come to London, Mom?"

"I told you, Cammie. I was detained."

It was the same phrase both Townsend and Professor Buckingham had used, but as I looked at my mother, I knew she hadn't missed her flight, been caught in a meeting, lost her passport. They had meant *detained* as in handcuffs and hard cots and facilities run by the CIA.

"Detained how? Detained where? Langley?" I watched the light change in my mother's eyes and knew that I was right.

"When an operative is accused of being a double agent, it's standard operating procedure for anyone associated with him or her to be questioned. It's protocol, kiddo. It's *nothing.*"

"What about the other teachers? Professor Buckingham? Mr. Smith? Why weren't they—"

"They were questioned, Cam. We were all questioned."

"Then why were you late? Why are *you* the only one just getting back to school now?"

"I've known Mr. Solomon the longest." She drew a deep breath. "I'm the one who hired him and brought him here, so naturally . . ." She trailed off. She didn't look at me for a long time. "But I'm back now." She caressed my hair. "You're safe." She pulled me to her, breathed deeply. "You're *safe.*"

There are things that go unsaid between people, lingering under the surface for decades, for lifetimes. I've wondered sometimes if spies have more of those things or fewer. More, I think. There are just too many things that even the bravest people in the world aren't brave enough to say out loud.

"Mr. Solomon came to me," I whispered.

My mother stepped away. "I know."

"He said they were wrong. He said he didn't do it—that they're after the wrong man. I . . ." I thought about the sadness in him as he'd hugged me. "I believed him."

"Joe Solomon is an amazing operative, sweetheart."

"So—"

"Amazing operatives make the best liars." She sank onto the leather couch, seeming almost too weak to stand. "He's never coming back, Cammie."

In the years since my father died, I've seen my mother cry once, maybe twice, and never when she knew I could see her. But in that moment, tears welled in her eyes, and I didn't know if she was speaking of Mr. Solomon or of my father as she whispered, "He's never coming back."

Chapter Eighteen

Gallagher Girls don't skip class. We don't play hooky, and there has never been a senior ditch day. Ever. But walking through the halls the next morning, I wanted to make an exception. I wanted to run—to hide like I'd never hidden before. To crawl back into bed and sleep a million years.

Turns out, I wasn't the only one.

"Good morning, Ms. Morgan."

I heard the floorboards creak behind me. I recognized the groggy voice. But the face that I saw when I turned wasn't quite what I was expecting.

Sure, Agent Townsend's hair was damp from a shower, and his clothes were fresh and neatly pressed, but his eyes were red and puffy. When he pushed past me and walked to his desk at the front of the room, he carried himself delicately, like a man who dearly wished the world would stop spinning. (His teeth, on the other hand, did seem significantly whiter.)

Note to self: never volunteer to help Elizabeth Sutton test one of her experiments.

The lights were off in the CoveOps classroom, but when Tina Walters paused by the door and reached for the switch, our teacher grumbled, "Leave them off."

As we made our way to our chairs, Townsend squeezed his eyes shut as if our footsteps were rifle shots in the dark.

"I don't care what you do with the next hour," he said softly, easing into the chair behind his desk. "I don't care how you do it. Just do it . . . *quietly*."

People have bad mornings at the Gallagher Academy all the time—yawning girls who have pulled all-nighters, aching bodies struggling to climb the stairs after a particularly hard week in P&E. The first time I met Agent Townsend, I'd wanted him to feel as badly as I felt; and standing there that morning, I thought maybe he did.

Especially when the lights suddenly flashed on and I heard my mother say, "Well, hello."

I saw him squint and jump—watched him turn to take in the woman by the door, but I don't know if surprise would be the right word to describe it.

"Welcome to the Gallagher Academy, Agent Townsend. We're so happy to have you here."

Note to self: Rachel Morgan is a totally awesome liar.

"I wanted to say hello at breakfast, but . . ." She studied his haggard face. "I can see that you perhaps needed to sleep in."

Townsend slowly turned his gaze toward me. "It must have been something I ate."

"I'm very sorry to hear that. Our chef usually gets nothing but rave reviews." Mom strolled across the front of the class-room. She kept her arms crossed, staring out the window, before slowly turning to the rest of the class. "Hello, girls."

There was a splattering of *hellos* and *welcome backs*, but for the most part we were quiet—waiting.

"I must say, when the Gallagher trustees told me that the CIA and MI6 had recommended you for the position, I was sur-prised. I hope the pace at our little school isn't too slow for you."

"No," he said, sinking to the corner of his desk. "If Joe Solomon can do it..."

I felt a flash of rage at the name, but if my mother felt the same, she didn't show it.

"And how are you finding things?" she asked. "Is there anything you need?"

"You mean besides access to the sublevels?"

My mother nodded. "Yes. Professor Buckingham has apprised me of the new safety concerns as far as the subs go. We're working on it."

"I see," Agent Townsend said, but the words sounded more like *yeah, right*.

Then a sort of shocked look crossed my mother's face.

"Oh, I'm sorry, Agent Townsend. Please, continue. Don't let me interrupt your lecture."

She took an empty seat in the front row on the far right side of the room, and it was Agent Townsend's turn to look surprised.

"I'm sorry, Mrs. Morgan. Are you . . . staying?"

"Yes," Mom said.

"Well, if I'd known, I would have prepared something special for the occasion."

My mother smiled. "Oh, whatever you had slated for today will be fine, I'm sure. I just like to pop in occasionally to hear all of our faculty teach. Please, don't let me stop you."

I heard Bex stifle a giggle. Tina Walters cut her eyes at me.

"Excellent," Townsend said with a smile. "You're just in time to begin our study of the Circle of Cavan."

Outside, the sky was a crisp, clear blue, but it felt like a storm was brewing inside our classroom. There was a static in the air so strong, I didn't dare touch anything—afraid I'd feel a spark.

He turned to look at Mom. "If that is okay with you, of course, Mrs. Morgan."

"That's something that would typically be covered in Professor Buckingham's senior level History of Espionage course, but given the circumstances, I think we can make an exception."

I expected her to look at me—smile at me—something, anything, besides turning to take in the entire class and saying, "You see, girls, Agent Townsend is something of a legend in the clandestine services. I can't think of anyone more qualified for this particular lecture."

"Even Joe Solomon?" I doubt any of my classmates saw the malicious gleam in Townsend's eyes.

I don't think they heard the anger in my mother's voice as she said, "No. Not even him."

And with that, Townsend spun on us. He sounded almost like a real teacher when he said, "The most important thing that any of you should know about the Circle of Cavan is that it is an organization composed almost entirely of other organizations' spies—I'm talking about double agents. Sleeper operatives. They have agents—traitors—at every level of every major security service in the world. They could be any-where . . ." He moved around his desk. "Even here."

I watched my classmates' eyes as the Circle became more than just some legend about Gilly and a ball gown and a trai-tor and a sword.

"Of course, they operate so deeply underground that some in the clandestine services think the Circle is nothing but a ghost story—an elaborate legend. But in the past hundred years alone, they have been behind at least five assassinations—that we know of—and they've been strong instigators of three wars. They have sold the identities of dozens of CIA and MI6 under-cover operatives to hostile governments, and they came closer than anyone outside the Secret Service will ever know to kill-ing a sitting president of the United States."

He crossed his arms and stared at us. "So make no mistake, they are *very real indeed*."

We sat there for fifteen minutes, listening to him cite facts as if the Circle was just another group or movement or cause —as if this wasn't personal.

"What do they want?" I heard myself asking.

"Money. Power. Control of—"

"*With me?*" I interrupted. "What do they want with me?"

I expected him to glance at my mother or avoid the question, but instead, he settled onto the corner of the desk. "That, we do not know. Yet." He paused. "Anything you'd like to add, Rachel?"

I thought she'd tell him that was enough, that class was over. But instead my mother crossed her long legs and placed her elbows on the desk. "Perhaps you could talk a little about their history."

He nodded. "Joseph Cavan was Irish by birth, and conventional wisdom holds that his followers retreated to his ancestral home after Gillian Gallagher allegedly killed him."

"Allegedly?" Bex said.

Townsend ignored her. "But now the Circle has strongholds in every corner of the world. It is important to understand that, unlike most political and religious-based groups, the Circle of Cavan has no cause—no calling or purpose beyond profit and power. They are large enough to be dangerous, and small enough to slip through cracks. They are mobile, careful, and very highly trained. And the scary thing is—for the most part—we're the ones who trained them."

"What does that mean?" Tina asked.

"It means I wasn't lying when I said they are almost always double agents," he snapped. "The Circle excels at isolating and recruiting agents who are young, vulnerable, or both."

"But how do you know?" Tina asked.

A sly smile slid over his face as he stood and studied us all in turn. "Because I'm the man who tracks them."

If we hadn't hated him a lot, we might have liked him a little at that moment. But we did. So we didn't.

"Make no mistake, girls, the Circle is dangerous not for what they are, but *who* they are. And *where* they are. And they could be anyone. They could be"—he turned to look at my mother—"*anywhere*."

Chapter nineteen

Number of hours I wandered around the mansion, going nowhere: 6

Number of secret passageways I looked for in the hopes of going somewhere: 27

Number of secret passageways I found that were actually still working: 1 (But it only went to the kitchen.)

Number of cookies I swiped while in the kitchen: 1 (Oh, okay, 3—but they were really little cookies.)

Number of times I wanted to cry: 9

Number of times I changed my mind: 9

And so I just kept walking—through the library with its rows of books and dying fire, past the elevator that could no longer take me to Sublevel Two. The halls were quiet and dark, as if the mansion itself were sleeping—resting up for a new day. And then I stopped at the Hall of History and stared at the sword of Cavan, realizing that, for the first time since November, I was actually alone.

Well...almost.

"Hello, Ms. Morgan." A deep voice cut through the darkness behind me.

Sure, it was two in the morning on a school night, but somehow I wasn't surprised when I turned and saw Mr. Smith. Well...actually...the fact that he was walking around in slippers and one of those old-fashioned nightshirts *did* surprise me; the fact that he was awake did not.

"I..." I started. Somehow, even though I technically wasn't doing anything wrong, I felt like I'd been caught. "I couldn't sleep."

"It's okay, Ms. Morgan." He came to stand beside me in the warm glow of the sword's glass case. Protective beams rippled through the room like waves.

I glanced at my teacher. Maybe it was the hour, or the fact that one of us was wearing a dress (and it wasn't me), but I dared to ask, "So what's your excuse?"

"A seasoned operative should always check his or her perimeter at unexpected times and in unexpected ways." I glanced at Mr. Smith's nightgown—I mean shirt...nightshirt. If *unexpected* was what it took to stay safe, then Mr. Smith was going to be alive forever. "You will do well to remember that, Cammie."

"Yes, sir." I stared at the sword. "Thank you. It's actually kind of nice..."

But then I trailed off. I didn't dare say what I was thinking.

"It's okay." There was a knowing wink in Mr. Smith's eye. "You can say it."

I glanced down at the floor. "It's nice getting some actual Covert Operations advice. I've missed it."

"Mr. Townsend is a fine operative, Cammie."

"Yes, of course, I didn't mean to imply—"

"Ambitious. Proud. Calculating . . . But he is perhaps not a natural for the classroom?"

"No," I agreed. "He'll never be as good as . . ." But I stopped short, suddenly unable to say the name aloud.

"No, he isn't what you're used to," Mr. Smith agreed.

"I believed him." I don't know where the words came from, but there, in the light of that sword, I simply had to set them free. "Joe Solomon is a liar. And a traitor. And I believed him. Even after London . . . He was talking crazy and I still—"

"Was he crazy, Cammie? Was he really?"

I looked at the most careful spy I'd ever known—stared up into the fifth face I'd seen him wear, and tried to focus on the eyes that hadn't changed since my first day of seventh grade.

"Joe Solomon is many things, Cammie. But crazy? Crazy is the one that I don't think I'll ever believe."

Mr. Smith took a step toward the Grand Staircase, the hem of his nightshirt swaying as he moved.

"Do try to get some sleep, Cammie. And good night."

Walking back upstairs that night, I thought of Mr. Smith's words and the way Mr. Solomon had gripped my hand at the Tower of London and pulled me through the dark. As I started up the old circular staircase that leads to the junior suites, cool air landed on my arms, and I looked out through the old wavy glass. It reminded me of the cold wind in London, the rippling waves of the Thames as it flowed below.

I remembered how lost Mr. Solomon had seemed as he hugged me on the bridge—how very strange and foreign the gesture had felt.

Where do men like Joe Solomon go when they fall? I asked myself. I wondered if there would be any help for him, waiting on the shore.

I took another step, but as I moved up the spiral stairs, something outside caught my eye. Something made me stop and stare out across the grounds.

Light from the mansion's windows streaked through the darkness, pebbling the dark, cloudy sky. And that was when I saw them—the birds that were sweeping out into the open air and then back again, stretching their wings.

For a moment, I stood still, listening to the howling wind and the faint cooing of the birds, and my teacher's words that had been playing over and over in my mind for weeks.

"Follow the pigeons."

Chapter Twenty

"**I**t's there!" My voice was cracking, and the words came in short gasps as if I were out of shape. Out of time. "Mr. Smith was right. *He isn't crazy!*"

I heard my roommates' footsteps on the stairs behind me, as Bex asked, "Cam, what are you talking about?"

"The pigeons!" I'm sure I must have looked like an insane person. And technically, I have been hit on the head *a lot*, so my roommates had good reason to look at each other as if all that brain trauma was bound to catch up with me eventually.

"Cam," Liz said slowly, her eyes still puffy from sleep. "Where are we going?"

Something was alive in me then. Maybe fear. Maybe dread. But mostly, I think it was hope as I climbed the stairs, higher and higher. When we reached the landing, I felt the cold air that seeped through the seams in the stone, and in that second my heart stopped. I stood, frozen by the cold stone beneath my fingers and a hope that I didn't dare to say, as I traced the rough carving of the bird in flight, and pushed.

The five largest stones receded, revealing a small compartment and a rusty lever.

"Cammie!" Liz exclaimed. "No. You're not supposed to leave the mansion! What are you doing?"

But she was too late, because the door was already swinging open, a rush of freezing wind was blowing against my face and across my bare legs, but I didn't feel the chill.

I just turned to look at my best friends, who stood in the light of the doorway, and said, "I'm following the pigeons."

We'd been here before, of course. Just a few months ago we'd sat on the dusty, overturned crates that were the last relics of the Gallagher Academy's once-proud covert carrier pigeon breeding program. We'd sat there for hours, looking out onto the lights of Roseville, talking about the people who were after Macey. After me. But now, the space looked totally different.

"What . . ." Liz started, looking around. "What is all this?"

Chalkboards lined the inner wall of the rampart, far away from the glassless windows that overlooked the grounds. The crates were stacked neatly to one side. A lone chair sat in the center of floor, facing the blackboards, as if someone had spent hours in that place, trying to solve an impossible equation.

"This must be what Mr. Solomon wanted us to find." I stepped closer to the blackboards that had Mr. Solomon's words scrawled over every inch. "He risked everything—just to tell me to find this," I said.

"Cammie . . ." Bex started. "You know as well as I do he was talking crazy. He wasn't Joe Solomon."

"But we're here," I snapped back. "It's not crazy if we're here."

What does it say?" Liz's voice was soft, her eyes focused as she stepped slowly closer to the board, and I knew she wasn't talking to us; her mind was lost in code, trying to see through the chaos.

"What is it, Liz?" Macey asked.

Liz shook her head. "I . . . I don't know. I've never seen anything quite like it."

"It's crazy, is what it is." Bex banged her fist against the board.

"Think about it, Bex. Think. He's one of the most wanted men on the planet, and I'm the world's best-guarded girl. Why come to me in London? If he's working for the Circle, why take that risk?"

"I don't know, Cam. Why did he kill your dad? Why did he join the Circle in the first place? Maybe he snapped or broke or . . ." I thought that she might cry. "Maybe this is what he is now."

"Was he crazy during finals week? Was he crazy in D.C.?" I felt Mr. Smith's words washing over me. "If he's not crazy, Bex, then he came to London for a reason." I threw out my arms and stepped closer to the boards. "He came to London for *this*."

The four of us were standing in the very place Joe Solomon had stood, staring at the words and numbers and diagrams that he'd written. There were answers here. Clues. He'd risked his freedom—his life—to bring me to this rooftop. I had followed the pigeons, and that night I stood without a coat in the freezing cold, trying to decipher what they had to say.

Behind me, a pigeon cawed. The sound was eerie and loud as I squinted through the dark toward the ledge. It cawed again.

"Stupid birds," Liz said, shooing her hands toward the lone pigeon that sat perched on the railing.

Most people don't know that anything can be a cutout, a go-between, a messenger for spies. This part of the mansion existed because pigeons had once been some of the best. They never talked when interrogated; even the best spy satellites in the world couldn't track them.

"Go on," Liz said again. "Get—"

"Wait," I said, reaching for my best friend's hand, staring at the small bird that sat stoically, waiting in the dark.

"Cam." Bex's voice was soft. "Cam, what is it?"

I inched toward the bird and reached for the tiny slip of paper wrapped delicately around its leg.

If you're reading this, you've found it. And if you've found it, you know. Must see you. Meet me at the place where we did the brush passes. Send me back the time.

Please come.

And please be careful.

The words were neatly typed. There was no signature—no name of any kind. And even though I knew it had been reckless to send it, reckless for me to read it—totally and completely foolish to even think about doing as it said—the truth of the matter is that a spy's life isn't about never taking chances. It's about taking chances that are worth the risk.

Chapter twenty-one

"What about the old ventilation shafts in the basement?" Bex asked as we sat beside a roaring fire in the library late the next night.

I shook my head. "Covered with eight inches of fresh concrete."

"The trick fireplace on the second floor?" Macey tried.

"Maybe." I considered the locks and bars that had been added over winter break. "Assuming we could get a blowtorch. Do any of you have a blowtorch?"

Liz perked up as if she were about to say that yes, she did have a blowtorch in the back of her closet.

"I'm afraid to know," I said, holding out my hand to stop her.

"Boy, they really want to keep us in, don't they?" Macey said.

"No." Bex shook her head and stared at me. "They want

to keep the Circle out." She waited a second, as the truth of the matter settled down on the three of us. "This is dangerous. *Too* dangerous."

"I'm with Bex," Macey said. "He's asking you to take a really big risk, Cam."

They were right, but all I could think about was the way he'd walked into the center of the very people who were scouring the world to find him. "Maybe it's my turn."

"Okay. Fine. Let's say it *isn't* true," Bex offered. "Let's say Mr. Solomon is innocent and wrongly accused and that he didn't kill . . ." She looked away, then back again. "Let's say he is the man we know. Does the Mr. Solomon *we* know tell you to sneak out of the Gallagher Academy, go into town, and meet up with a known fugitive? Does Joe Solomon tell you to be stupid?"

The answer was obvious. That was probably why none of us said it.

"Why don't *we* go?" Liz said, pointing to herself and Bex and Macey. "See him. Get the message. Bring it back."

"I can't explain it, guys," I said, shaking my head. "I just know I've got to go."

"That doesn't mean you have to be stupid!" Bex shot back, and I realized that *Bex* was being cautious. *Bex* had become the voice of reason. "You didn't see it, Cammie," she went on. "You didn't have to watch them drug you and drag you away like a doll. You were there, Cam, but you didn't have to watch your friend almost go away forever. You don't know how that feels."

"Yeah," Macey said softly. "She *does.*"

I looked at the girls I would trust with my life. Then I thought about my dad and the man he'd probably trusted with his.

"I have to go," I said. "It's my mission."

"You're *our* mission," Bex countered.

"What are we saying?" Liz exclaimed. "Cam, we don't have to sneak out. We don't even have to go by ourselves. I bet your mom—"

"No," I said, cutting her off. "If she got caught helping Joe Solomon . . . No. We're on our own."

"I know, Cam," Bex said, stopping me. "I know. But if we do this without backup—"

"What if they're wrong, Bex?" I pleaded. "What if he's the only chance we'll ever have at finding out what happened to my dad? What if while everyone is chasing him, no one is trying to stop the Circle? *What if he didn't do it?*"

Bex's voice was flat and calm and strong as she looked at me. "What if he did?"

Chapter Twenty-two

Covert Operations Report
The Operatives utilized a basic Trojan horse
scenario. If, instead of a horse, you substitute a
1987 Dodge Minivan.

Well, it turns out that when one of the world's most dangerous
and covert terrorist organizations is after one of your students,
school officials care less about keeping people *in* than they care
about keeping people *out*.

Or at least that's what Bex and Macey and I told ourselves
as we crawled beneath a tarp, a blanket, and about ten million
physics notebooks, and lay as quietly as possible in the back of
Liz's van.

"Where to this evening?" the guard at the front gate asked.
I could picture him leaning against the driver's side window,
chomping on his gum.

I had to hold my breath as I waited for the soft, Southern voice that answered, "Just a road check, Walter."

"What's she up to now, Lizzie?" the guard asked. In the light that crept in through the weave of the blanket, I saw that Bex was holding her breath too.

"Almost four hundred miles per gallon," Liz blurted. "I mean three ninety-five to be specific—which I can be. Specific, that is. You know me, Walter. I'm a very detail-oriented person. I'm just going out to test it in stop-and-go driving. I'm not hiding anything!" she blurted, and Bex's eyes went wide.

———

PROS AND CONS OF BREAKING OUT OF SCHOOL
(A list by Operatives Morgan, McHenry, and Baxter)

PRO: As Trojan horse operations go, the back of a mini-van isn't nearly as bad as it can get.

CON: Rebecca Baxter, despite her many good qualities, is a cover hog.

PRO: There's nothing like a completely unsupervised, possibly illegal covert operation to take a girl's mind off the terrorist organization that is after her—not to mention her Culture & Assimilation homework.

CON: The girl really should have been doing her Culture & Assimilation homework.

PRO: When you haven't had a real CoveOps lesson in months, you'll take any practical experience you can get.

CON: When you haven't had a real CoveOps lesson in months, you can't help but feel really, really rusty.

––––––––

I know the streets of Roseville. I've walked them with my classmates. I've held hands on them with my first (and technically only) boyfriend. I've seen them filled with football fans and parade spectators, with ladies selling cakes and candies for the church auxiliary, and kids out for a Saturday matinee.

It's as all-American as a town can possibly be, with its white gazebo and movie marquee and town square, but it seemed different as I stood in the library bell tower, staring down at the square. There was nothing there but me and sky—no walls, no guards—and yet I felt stranded. Like the ravens, I knew I couldn't fly away.

"You have good cover here," Bex told me.

I could hear Macey through the comms unit in my ear, saying what I already knew: "The square is clear." I could see Liz in the van, circling the block.

"Liz is tracking you from the van," Bex said. "We've got backup relays outside of town in case the van is compromised."

Bex kept talking, but all I could think of was how the air was colder. The stars felt brighter. The breeze was softer as it blew against my cheek. It was as if all my senses were in overdrive, and I couldn't help but think most people feel like that sometimes—when they're alone or in the dark. When they hear a noise in the closet or a creak on the floorboards, they sense it. It's not about being scared—it's about being alive. The nerves work harder, carrying messages to the brain, getting it ready for fight or flight, and that night, well, let's just say that night my nerves had their work cut out for them.

"Cam?" Bex asked as if I hadn't heard her. But she was wrong. That night I heard and saw and smelled *everything*. "I'm gonna get into position. Are you satisfied with this position?"

I scanned the square and nodded. "Yes."

"You're safe here." She touched my arm almost as if she were trying to get my scent, as if she might soon be chasing me around the world.

And then I watched her go.

Standing alone in the tower, I reminded myself of all the things in the world that I knew to be absolutely true: Rebecca Baxter was the best spy at the Gallagher Academy and the absolute last person who would lie about my safety. I had GPS trackers in my watch, my shoes, my ponytail holder, and my stomach (thanks to a new edible model Liz had been trying out).

My roommates and I all carried panic buttons that could summon an army within the blink of an eye. They could track me anywhere in the world (and, Liz firmly believed, the moon).

And yet I couldn't shake the feeling that the square seemed smaller from where I stood, or maybe the world just felt bigger.

I held a pair of binoculars to my eyes and scanned the streets, telling myself that I was as safe as I could possibly be. I was prepared. I could handle anything. I was ready for everything. . . .

Except for the sight of a tall figure with broad shoulders, appearing as if from nowhere at the edge of the gazebo, and saying, "Hello, Gallagher Girl."

Chapter twenty-three

Perspective is a powerful thing. Seriously. I *highly* recommend it. There are things you just can't see unless you take a good step back and watch very, very closely.

I mean, if I'd been standing in the town square and not the bell tower, I might have heard the girl say, "Well, hello yourself," but I might have missed the way the boy stumbled backward as she turned. I might not have noticed the way his shoulders fell and his head jerked in the manner of someone who had not found what he was looking for.

I might never have realized that Zach was disappointed to find another girl in the gazebo.

"Macey?" Zach asked as if he couldn't believe his eyes, which was maybe the most flattering thing ever, because *no one* has ever mistaken me for Macey McHenry. Ever. But it was dark, and even without access to the world's greatest closet for deception and disguise, Macey was still the daughter of a cosmetics heiress. And in a wig and Zach's old jacket, she made for a good decoy, or at least good enough.

"Where's Cammie?" Zach asked.

"You look disappointed to see me, Zach," Macey teased. "Don't you like my jacket?"

"Where is she?" Zach demanded.

"At school," Macey lied without missing a beat. "Watching from a live video feed. She's *safe*." She inched closer, staring up at him.

"The jammers at the school wouldn't allow that, Macey. Now, where is she?" He turned. "I know she's around here somewhere," he said, scanning the alleys and buildings that lined the square.

"She's safe where she is, Zach." Bex stepped out of the darkened alcove by the movie theater and moved into place behind him. "And we're going to keep her that way."

"I need to talk to her," he told them.

"So talk," Macey said. "We've got comms. She can hear you."

"I need to *see* her."

"I'm coming down," I blurted, desperate to be off the sidelines, but Bex's hand was on her ear. She was shouting at me.

"You stay where you are!"

But I was already gone.

"She's lucky to have you," Zach said after a long time. "She needs you."

"What are you doing here, Zach?" Macey asked, but Zach only shook his head. He looked down at the ground.

"It's complicated."

"So un-complicate it." Even as I said the words, I knew I might regret them. And soon. Maybe Zach was bait and I was walking into a trap. Maybe Bex would save the Circle the trouble and kill me on the spot, but I couldn't stay away.

"You're with him," I said.

"Technically, he's on an errand halfway around the world right now," Zach tried to joke, but my mind raced on.

"Liz and Macey told me that just because you go to Blackthorne doesn't mean . . ." My voice caught. "But you really are with him."

"Gallagher Girl, listen to me."

"So . . . what happened, Zach? Did the Circle recruit you too?"

He looked at me for a long time before he lowered his head and whispered, "Not exactly."

At the edge of the square, a streetlight flickered. Shadows crept across the grass for a split second, and I flinched, remembering the last time I'd been alone with Zach and the lights had gone out. I remembered the sound of a gunshot and the sight of my aunt falling to the dark street, while one of the Circle's agents stood between me and freedom. But instead of firing, he had looked at Zach and said, "*You?*"

"What are you doing here, Zach?" I asked, my throat suddenly too dry.

"He asked me to get a message to you."

"So *send* me a message! What was so important that I had

to risk my friends' safety to sneak out here?" I demanded. "Huh? What was so—"

"I had to *see* you." He closed the space between us. His hands were warm from his pockets as they closed around my fingers. "I had to know that you were okay. I had to see you and touch you and . . . know."

He brushed my hair away from my face, his fingers light against my skin. "In London . . ." He trailed off. "After D.C. . . ."

"I'm fine," I said, easing away. "CAT scans and X-rays were normal. No lasting damage."

Most people believe me when I lie. I've learned how to say the words just right. I have a trusting kind of face. But the boy in front of me was a trained operative, so Zach knew better. And besides, Zach knew me.

"Really?" He touched my face again. " 'Cause I'm not."

I don't know Zachary Goode. I've touched him and spoken to him and felt his lips on mine, but I don't know him—not really.

I could feel the clock ticking and knew that the girl I'd been the year before was officially out of time.

"I'm fine, Zach," I said, pulling away. "But I've got to go. We only have a half hour before they miss us."

He pointed to the darkness. "Who else is out there?"

"The usuals," I said, still not wanting to give away too much.

"Your mom?" he asked, but I didn't have to say anything—he read the answer in my eyes. "Good," Zach said. "He doesn't want her taking the risk."

"What does he care? If he cared about her, then..." I trembled.

"So they told you?" he asked, stepping away.

"Yeah. They told me he's part of the Circle, and he...My father is dead because of him." My heart was pounding hard inside my chest. My throat was on fire. "Is this the part where you deny it?"

"No." Zach shook his head. "It's the part where I ask a favor."

"You've got a lot of nerve," Bex said, moving closer, but Zach's gaze never left mine.

"There's a book, Gallagher Girl," he said, then swallowed. "It might be the only thing in the world the Circle wants as much as they want you."

"What kind of book?" I asked.

"A journal. Joe—Mr. Solomon—needs you to read it."

"Why?" I asked.

"It explains everything, Gallagher Girl. And besides, if he doesn't make it out of this...He needs *you* to read it."

"Where is it?" Bex asked.

"You're not going to like it. It's risky and—"

"Where is it?" Bex, Macey, and I demanded in unison.

"Sublevel Two."

"The subs?" Bex shook her head. "No. Can't. They're closed. Off-limits."

"Oh, and off-limits has always stopped you before?" Zach asked her. "Look, they're not technically closed—they're just rigged to explode if anyone goes near them," he said as if we encounter highly dangerous explosives every day. And . . . well . . . we sort of do.

"How do you know about the subs?" I asked, already sure of the answer.

"Because a week before I saw you in London, Joe heard the CIA had a source who'd started talking. He had to get off the grid and stay off the grid—fast. They were coming for him, Gallagher Girl, and he couldn't risk getting caught down there, so . . ."

Zach took a deep breath and smiled his most mischievous smile. "I know about the subs because Joe Solomon's the one who rigged them."

Chapter twenty-four

Joe Solomon didn't booby-trap the sublevels of the Gallagher Academy for Exceptional Young Women to explode or implode or fill up with water from the lake.

Don't get me wrong, all of those things could *totally* happen! But no matter what you might have heard, Mr. Solomon didn't put those protocols in place—the Gallagher Academy trustees did, a long, long time ago. Before I was born. Before my mother was born. After all, when you have that many covert secrets in one place, it's important to protect them. And if the protection measures fail, it's important to destroy them.

So I really wish people would get it straight: Mr. Solomon *did not* build the triggers that would destroy the subs!

He's just the one who turned them on.

Or at least that's what Zach told us.

And that . . . Yeah, that was the problem.

"What's wrong?" Liz asked, despite the fact that, at the front of the room, Dr. Fibs and Madame Dabney were in the midst of an incredibly interesting joint lecture on secret writing techniques (and why a Gallagher Girl should really learn how to make her own invisible ink and do calligraphy).

"Is it the sensors in the elevator shafts?" she guessed.

I shook my head.

"The two-second delay before the anti-invasion protocols kick on and we get . . . smushed?"

"Oh my!" Dr. Fibs cried. I looked up to see that he had accidentally spilled his latest invisibility concoction over Madame Dabney, and that her white blouse was becoming more and more invisible by the second.

"I know what you're thinking, Cam," Liz went on. "We've been looking for a way into . . . *you know where* . . . for weeks and we aren't any closer. But that's not exactly true!"

At the front of the room, Madame Dabney (who, by the way, wears way sexier bras than anyone would have guessed) started dabbing at the front of her blouse with an antique tablecloth, and Dr. Fibs reached for a lighter.

"Now, remember, girls, the ink becomes visible again when exposed to heat!" Dr. Fibs yelled as he flicked the lighter on and the tablecloth went up in flames in Madame Dabney's hands.

"We have an entry strategy and an exit strategy and . . . we have a lot of strategies!" Liz said, her eyes wide, and right then I knew that a part of Liz didn't care that Zach and Mr. Solomon had asked us to do something that no one had ever done in a hundred and fifty years. To Liz, it was just a puzzle, a test. And Liz is very, very good at tests.

"Yeah, Cam," she said again as soon as the smoke cleared

(literally) and we were gathering our things and leaving class. "We'll figure it out."

"Figure what out?" Bex asked, falling into step beside us.

"Nothing," I whispered.

"Wrong answer," Bex said, leaning closer, her voice barely audible through the cascade of girls that filled the halls. "Now what's wrong?"

"Zach," Macey guessed with a shrug. She eyed me. "It's got to be Zach, right?"

"So the subs' next-generation cameras with the 360 degree range and heat-sensitive triggers *aren't* bothering you?" Liz asked. I couldn't tell if she was mocking me or not.

"There's something he's not telling us," I whispered.

"Like what?" Bex asked, interested again.

Like what's so important about this journal? Like why didn't that man in D.C. shoot him and kidnap me when he had the chance? At least a dozen questions filled my mind, but the halls were crowded, and there was only one thing I dared to say.

"There's just . . . something."

"He's a guy, Cam." Macey pushed past me and led the way down the hall. "And a spy. He's a guy spy. There's always going to be something he's not telling."

"He fought with us—in D.C.," Liz said. There was no doubt in her voice, no fear. "I know you couldn't see, Cam. I know they drugged you and you banged your head and all. But he and Mr. Solomon both fought *with* us," Liz said one final time, and then turned and ran toward Mr. Mosckowitz's classroom.

I turned to Macey.

"So he's mysterious," she said with a shrug. "Mysterious is *sexy*." And then it was her turn to spin on her heels and run out the front doors, on her way to P&E.

When I turned to Bex, I wanted her to say that everything was going to be fine—that there was nothing the four of us couldn't do, and it was just a matter of time until we found our way into Sublevel Two, cleared Mr. Solomon's name, and stopped global warming (not necessarily in that order).

I looked at her. I waited.

"We can't trust him." She pushed past me, stepped calmly into Room 132. "We can't trust anyone."

I wanted to tell her she was wrong (but she wasn't). I thought I might think of a way to prove he was an exception (but I couldn't). I wanted her to stop looking at me as a spy and start talking to me as a girl, but Gallagher Girls are only exceptional because we're both—all the time. I wanted to go into the CoveOps classroom and pretend to read whatever boring book Townsend was going to give us and replay every conversation that Zach and I had ever had. But before I could take a single step, Agent Townsend appeared in the doorway of the classroom, a coat in his hands, saying, "Junior class, come with me."

I know we're supposed to be in the business of being prepared for anything—of never, ever being surprised—but let me tell you, most of the people I know still shock the fire out of me on a regular basis. (Like, for example, the time Mr. Mosckowitz and Liz went rock climbing together and neither of them actually died.) But in five and a half years at the world's premiere school for spies, very few things have surprised me more than walking with the rest of the junior CoveOps class, following Agent Townsend through the halls.

He was the sort of man who always moved with purpose, never a wasted step, but that day he walked even faster. He seemed taller. And though we were still inside the Gallagher mansion, something told me that Agent Townsend was finally back on familiar ground.

"Um...sir..." Tina Walters said, pushing through the crowd, trying to get as close as possible to the man at the front of the pack. "Are we going back to Sublevel Two?" she asked, but Townsend acted as if she hadn't uttered a single word.

"The primary job of any field agent is what?" he asked in a manner that made him sound almost like a real teacher. Almost.

"To recruit, run, and maintain assets of intelligence," Mack Morrison said, quoting page twelve from the old copy of *Understanding Espionage: A Beginner's Guide to Covert Operations, Third Edition*, that we'd all taken turns reading under the covers in the seventh grade.

Agent Townsend looked at her. I thought for a split second that he might actually smile, but instead he just said, "Wrong."

It felt like the entire class missed a step. Townsend, on the other hand, kept walking.

"The primary job of a field agent is to *use* people—strangers, typically. Sometimes friends. Secretaries, neighbors, girlfriends, boyfriends, janitors, and little old ladies crossing the street. We use them all."

He stopped in the center of the foyer and turned to face us, while, behind him, the main doors flew open. A van sat idling in the center of the drive. I was tempted to close my eyes and pretend that it was a real CoveOps lecture, that we had a real CoveOps teacher again.

But then Townsend said, "But, of course, if that's somehow beneath a Gallagher Girl . . ."

"No, sir!" Tina chanted.

He stepped aside and gestured toward the open doors. "Then, after you."

What happened next was a rush of emotion and adrenalin like I hadn't felt in weeks. It was intoxicating. I felt almost drunk. And yet I stayed still, watching my classmates race out the door and toward the waiting van.

"I suppose you think this is optional, Ms. Morgan?" Agent Townsend stood staring at me through the open door.

"Of course I want to go, but there are these security protocols"—I glanced away, somehow unable to face him as I admitted, "Professor Buckingham told me I'm not allowed to leave the grounds."

"And I suppose you think I've forgotten that fact?"

"No, sir."

"Then you think I'm a fool."

"No, sir, I—"

"Don't worry, Ms. Morgan, I know you're *special*. And because of you and your mother, I've spent a great deal of time and energy making *special* arrangements," he said with a condescending smirk. "But if you want to stay in the mansion..."

I didn't wait for him to finish. I was already out the door.

Chapter twenty-five

Spies need covert operations. I know it sounds crazy, but it's true. Because even though our brains are . . . you know . . . brain-sized, every undercover operative knows that a mind is totally big enough to get lost inside—to go crazy if you're left with too much time and too much room to let your biggest fears run free.

So, yeah. Spies *need* covert operations. And as I sat next to Bex in the Gallagher Academy van that was carrying us through the tall, metal gates that had stood between me and the world outside, I had to ask, "Do you hear that?"

"What?" she asked. "A little voice telling you you'd be better off staying where you bloody well were?"

"Nope." I smiled. "Freedom."

She looked at me like I might have been crazier than usual, but I didn't care.

I was riding in a van! (And in an actual seat this time, which, let me tell you, you really don't miss till it's gone.)

I was outside of school!

I was going on a mission!

I was going to...

Then I glanced out the window and realized I didn't have a clue where we were going.

And that totally made it better.

For two hours we rode in silence; the only sound was the hum of the van and the occasional snore (yes, actual *snoreage*) as Townsend slumped in the front seat, sleeping.

As the road stretched out before us and the trip got longer and longer, I'm pretty sure I wasn't the only Gallagher Girl in that van to feel acutely aware of three important facts. 1) We were missing lunch. 2) It's kinda hard to look like a super-tough, super-skilled superagent when your stomach's growling. And 3) We hadn't had a real Covert Operations lesson in months.

I stretched my arms out in front of me and thought I felt a creak. Rusty didn't even begin to cover it.

And then the van made a hard right turn, and Townsend bolted upright.

"Good," he said, without even a glance out the window. "We're here."

In case I haven't mentioned it before, I go to a *boarding school*. With gates. And walls. Plaid skirts and strict teachers. So while my classmates and I might be used to spending all of our time in a place that is exciting and semi-dangerous and full of incredibly delicious food, I couldn't remember a single time when I'd been in a place like *this*.

"Oh my gosh," Tina Walters said, summing up the reaction

of probably every single girl in the van at that particular moment. "Is that . . ."

But before she could finish, Agent Townsend threw open the doors and Tina's words got lost in the deafening roar of a roller coaster barreling along its tracks and people screaming at the top of their lungs as the ride quickly plunged, then rose again.

Somehow, sitting in the back of the van, I sort of knew exactly how they felt.

"All right," our teacher said ten minutes later in the manner of a man who just wanted to get it over with and go back to sleep, "everybody gets a target. Everybody gets a goal. Everybody gets an hour."

While he spoke, his gaze swept around the entrance of the amusement park as if no place filled with that many tourists and empty calories could ever leave him *amused*.

"These are decent people, I suppose. But the world is full of decent people with useful information, and to them we must lie—from them we must steal. If anybody has a problem with that . . . well, if you've got a problem with that, you would be well advised to choose another occupation."

He was right, of course. There's no softer way to put it. We get close to secretaries so we can bug their bosses' offices. We befriend widows so we can conduct surveillance on their neighbors' backyards. We are in the human intelligence business, and most of the people that we need to do our jobs are just people who happen to be in the wrong place at the wrong time.

So we tell lies and pick pockets and, most of all, we *use*.

"You," Agent Townsend said, pointing at Mack. "There's a forty-year-old man behind you with a blue ball cap."

"Yes, sir," Mack said, but she didn't turn to look in the man's direction.

"Do you see him?" Agent Townsend asked, frustrated.

"Yes, sir. Blue cap, green polo, navy backpack." Mack pointed at the reflection of the man that gleamed in the window behind our teacher's head. He glanced back and saw it, and for a split second—nothing more—I thought he might have been impressed. Maybe.

"Okay," Agent Townsend said slowly, "that man just put a piece of paper in the outer pocket of the bag. I don't care how you do it, but you need to find out what's written on that piece of paper."

Mack didn't need to be told twice. She turned on her heel and set off through the crowd, while I turned to study the man she was tailing.

"Wow, he really fits in," I admitted. "I never would have guessed he's CIA."

"He's not," Townsend said simply, still scanning the people who filled the park. "There, Ms. Walters," he said, pointing at an older lady riding an electric scooter.

"Is *she* from Langley?" Tina asked.

"I have no idea where she's from." Our teacher shrugged. "What I do know is that she just put her credit card in her purse, and it's your job to get me that number."

"But she's not an operative...." Tina hesitated. "She doesn't know it's an assignment.... So if I get caught..."

Townsend stared at her. "Then don't get caught."

It was still a game, I knew, but for the first time in the history of our exceptional education, the players on the other side didn't know we were playing. One by one, our classmates got their assignments until Bex and I were alone with our teacher.

"Baxter," Agent Townsend said, turning to Bex, "do you think you can find out the serial numbers of the five-dollar bill the man working the Tilt-A-Whirl just put into that lockbox?"

The look on her face said that yes, she *did* think she could find out, and yet she didn't turn to walk away. She waited as our teacher's gaze landed on me.

"And I guess that leaves us with Cammie Morgan." He slowly scanned the crowd. "I think maybe we'll find something especially fitting for you."

I didn't know what to say, so I stood quietly, waiting.

"There." He pointed toward a man in an official theme-park jumpsuit. "The keys on his belt—bring me an impression of at least three of them."

He smiled like he was so smart. I shrugged like it was so easy. Then, with my best friend beside me, I turned and started through the crowd.

Although it pains me to admit it, for his very first lesson, Agent Townsend had managed to bring us to one of the most challenging places a spy could ever be. After all, Mr. Solomon had

141

spent the last year and a half training us to see everything, hear everything, notice everything. And as I walked through the park, it was almost too much for my highly trained senses to take.

"Ooh!" I exclaimed, craning my neck as we walked past a stand selling some kind of deep-fried delicious on a stick. "I want one of those!"

"We don't have any money, Cam."

"Ooh, I want to ride that!"

"We only have an hour."

"I want—"

"I want you to take this seriously, okay?" Bex said, whirling on me.

"You sound like your mother," I said.

She practically glowed. "Thank you."

"Bex..." I said slowly. "I'm fine."

"You say that—"

"Bex." I cut her off and stopped in the center of the main avenue that snaked through the entire park. "Weren't you supposed to be following that guy?" I pointed to the attendant pushing a cart full of lockboxes in the opposite direction.

"I'm good where I am," she said.

"Bex..."

"Cammie..."

"Spot the surveillance," I told her.

"What?"

I thought back to the way her parents had led us all

around London—the game we hadn't played in weeks. *"Spot the surveillance."*

"Man selling balloons by the bumper cars," she said, not even blinking.

"The woman with the cotton candy," I added, pointing at just one of the guards that surrounded me at every turn.

It was her turn, but I couldn't shake the feeling that the game was over. We'd stopped keeping score on a bridge overlooking the Thames.

"By my count, there are thirteen operatives tailing me right now. And those are just the ones I've made. There are cameras every hundred yards, and if I'm not mistaken, a Blackhawk helicopter just did a flyby."

"*Two* Blackhawks," Bex corrected. "In a rotation."

"See? I'm fine," I said, and for the first time in a long time I meant it. I really did. It was as if the walls of my school had been picked up and transported here. It was like my school, but with cotton candy. No wonder I couldn't hold back a smile as I asked, "Do you think my mom would let Townsend bring me here if this place wasn't the Fort Knox of family fun?" Bex opened her mouth to speak, but I didn't give her the chance. "Go," I said.

For a moment she just stood there, watching. Waiting. Then my best friend turned away without another word.

For the next twenty minutes I walked alone in the busy park —past lines of people waiting to ride the Ferris wheel and buy cotton candy, through the crowd that had gathered around Eva Alvarez as she shot ninety-seven little mechanical ducks in a row. Roller coasters roared overhead with their screaming masses and screeching tracks. Wheels spun, fountains splashed, and the smell of people and junk food and heat wafted all around me until I wondered if I might be sick, overdosed on freedom.

So when the man with the clipboard walked off the main thoroughfare, I didn't mind.

Even though a girl in a private school uniform should probably stand out in a busy, public place, I was still the Chameleon, and I followed at the same easy pace and comfortable distance that had been bred into my DNA (a fact that Liz had once tried to verify in the lab, which led to the "no more blood samples this semester" rule of sophomore year).

When I wanted to stop to watch the jugglers, I watched. When I wanted to make faces at myself in the funhouse mirrors, I did. When I wanted to try something called a Waffle Burger, I cursed myself for not keeping an emergency twenty in my sock, like Grandma Morgan always taught me, and just kept walking. The man in the jumpsuit remained a constant figure in the corner of my eye.

I should probably point out that in all that time, the man never turned around. Not once did he check his tail. I was starting to think that this was the easiest covert operations lesson ever, when he slipped through a small gate in the fence that ran behind the merry-go-round, but I didn't hesitate. I didn't wait. I just did what I was born to do: I followed, knowing that whatever guards were following *me* would be quick to do the same.

It was quieter there, behind the barricades. A large man-made lake stretched out beside me. The smells of corn dogs and popcorn were lost beneath the scent of oil and grease. The bright lights and spinning wheels of the park were gone, replaced by a maze of carefully placed trees and perfectly engineered scaffolding that stretched high into the sky, blocking out the sun.

I thought of all the things I might say if someone saw me: I was there to meet my boyfriend. My classmates had sent me on a dare. I'd seen a stray animal come this way and it had appeared to be hurt.

So I wasn't afraid when the man stopped and opened the door of a long building that sat hidden in the midst of the park. I waited ten seconds, then followed, praying the door's hinges wouldn't squeak as I pulled it slowly open and stepped inside.

Christmas decorations lined one wall, and Fourth of July sparklers and banners covered the other. There were broken, faded bumper cars and log ride relics, and a statue of a clown. It was like a graveyard—where amusement came to die.

And that was the thought that filled my mind as I eased down the center aisle—soaking in the sights and smells and sounds that filled the air around me. Every fiber in my training and my gut wound together to tell me that the workman was gone—lost, out of sight.

But then I heard the faint scruff of heavy shoes on concrete and knew I was anything but alone.

"You *really* shouldn't be here."

Chapter twenty-six

The first time any of us had ever seen Joe Solomon, we'd thought he was a highly trained operative, a seasoned CoveOps veteran and...well...hot. But a year and a half later I barely recognized my teacher in the man who stood behind me. His face was drawn and pale. His hair was longer, his clothes grungier, but it was his eyes that had changed the most as he stepped toward me and demanded, "Cammie, you have to come with me. You have to come right now!"

As he reached for me, I jerked away. I didn't know whether to hug him or hit him (a feeling that I frequently associate with Blackthorne Boys, to tell you the truth), so I just shook my head. "No."

"Cammie, if *I* heard you were going to be here, then *they'll* know you're here. I have to get you out of here. Now!"

"It's true, isn't it?"

"The Circle could be here any second."

"You *are* the Circle!"

Joe Solomon had had far more practice telling lies than I've had trying to detect them, but I could see the truth in his eyes.

"It *is* true, isn't it?" I asked, even though, deep down, I knew it wasn't really a question. Even though *I knew*.

"I'm sorry, Cammie." He ran his hand through his hair. "Cammie, I'm so—"

"No," I said numbly. I felt myself backing away, my left hand tracing the cinder-block wall of the building. I scanned the room, looking for a piece of pipe or a tool—a weapon of any kind.

"Cammie, listen to me. I'll explain everything, but if my sources are right, then you're not safe here. You have to come with me."

"I'm not going anywhere with *you!*"

I wasn't thinking about the guards, who, moments before, I had been sure were watching my every move. I didn't reach for the panic button that I wore around my wrist like a watch, or call into my comms unit for help. I *wasn't* thinking as I brought my hand up along the side of his face—hard.

It was just a slap—nothing special. Hardly something they would ever teach in P&E. And yet I felt like doing it again. And again.

"I'm not going anywhere with you!" I said, striking out. "I'm not. I'm not. I'm..." I stopped and stared at him. "How could you?"

"I was young, Cammie."

"You were *my* age! And then you grew up and..." I didn't want to cry, and so I screamed. "You killed him!"

I expected him to lash back, strike me down where I stood. He was bigger, stronger, and more experienced, but rage is a force of its own. I watched him stumble back as if he knew that—as if I scared him.

"He's dead because of you!" I yelled, stepping forward, but Mr. Solomon didn't brace to block the blow.

Instead, he leaned against the wall, his eyes deeper and darker and sadder than anything I've ever seen, as my father's best friend stared at me, voice cracking, and whispered, "I know."

What happened next was a scene I've played and replayed in my mind a thousand times. I'll probably play it a thousand more. All I know for certain is that one second, a man I had revered, trusted, loved, and hated (in that order) was in front of me, crumbling. And in the next moment, time seemed to freeze as the door to the building swung open and a long shadow sliced across the concrete floor, and I heard a woman say, "He said we'd find you here."

I remember everything about my trip to Boston last summer—the sight of the balloons, the sounds of the crowds, and most of all, the way a masked woman and two men walked toward me through the spinning shadows of a helicopter's blades.

"No," I said, as if that simple word could stop it from happening again.

The woman looked so calm as she stood in the open doorway, as if nothing could go wrong this time. As if it were over.

I reached for my watch, punched the button again and

again, not daring to calculate the odds of beating the Circle for a third time—not willing to waste one second more.

"No!" I yelled. It didn't matter that she was older and taller and probably far more experienced—I charged toward her, knowing that my only hope lay on the other side of that open door.

But then I stopped, because the woman was no longer alone. Agent Townsend was there. Agent Townsend was looking at Joe Solomon and me as if Christmas had come early.

"You were right," the woman told Agent Townsend with a smile. "This was almost too easy."

I looked from the woman I could have sworn had been in Boston, to my new teacher. It didn't make sense, but sense was the last thing in the world that I could worry about, because Joe Solomon was rushing past me, flying through the open door. In one fluid motion, he knocked Townsend and the woman to the ground.

I rushed outside and saw the three of them rolling down a hill, fighting through the dirt and the weeds. Dust swirled around me, and standing there, I realized I had no idea whom to trust. All I really knew for certain is that sometimes all an operative gets is one second—nothing more.

And I had already started to run.

Chapter Twenty-Seven

It was a trap. It was a trap. It was a trap.

The words echoed in my mind, keeping rhythm with my feet as they hit the ground.

"Bex!" I yelled as I ran through the tall trees that grew up around the roller coaster. Far above me, people were flying through the sky, but down below, there was only static in my comms unit, and the rough ground that no tourist was ever supposed to see. I hurtled over spotlights and dodged cables as I bolted to the top of a hill, not once allowing myself to think about Mr. Solomon or the woman or Agent Townsend. I just kept running—toward the lake, toward the fence, toward help.

It was a trap.

At the top of the hill I could hear the sounds of the park floating across the lake. All I had to do was keep running, keep fighting, but then I saw them—the agents who had been in the crowd all day—following me, watching my every move. They were descending through the woods—emerging from behind the tall trees and the roller coaster's massive pillars, rushing past me.

Past me?

Not a soul tried to usher me to safety. And in that moment I knew that they weren't protectors. They were hunters. And me? I was the bait.

It was a trap.

I heard footsteps behind me, hard and fast.

"Zach," I called to the boy who was running toward me.

"Where is he?" Zach yelled, out of breath. I lunged forward and grabbed him. "Let me go, Gallagher Girl. I have to—"

"Do you want them to take you too?" I shouted, shaking him. When he stopped fighting I held him tighter. "They have him, Zach." I heard my mother's words coming back to me. "He's gone."

Mr. Solomon lay on the ground in the clearing below, bloody and bound, while agents still swarmed from all directions. I remembered how, once on a helicopter en route to Ohio, Mr. Solomon had told us that often the hardest thing an operative can do is nothing. Standing there that day, I knew that it was true—that Joe Solomon was always right.

"Stupid!" Zach yelled. He banged his hand hard against the trunk of a tree, and I couldn't tell whether the hand or the tree got the worst of it. He turned to me. "What happened?"

"CoveOps exercise. I tailed a man here. And then Mr. Solomon was there, talking about the Circle, saying I was in danger. And then there was a woman. I thought she was the woman from Boston."

"That wasn't her, Cammie."

"I know that now."

He grasped my shoulders. I could see a kind of fear settle into his eyes as he whispered, "There's no way Joe Solomon would ever be with *her*."

The roller coaster roared overhead, and I felt the ground vibrate beneath my feet.

"Why would he come here?" I asked. "It was a trap. Joe Solomon walked into a trap." Believe it or not, of all the things I'd seen and heard since London, that was what surprised me most of all.

"You." Zach sounded almost amazed that I didn't know. "If he thought you were going to be here—virtually unprotected ...There's nowhere he wouldn't go to save you."

"Why would he do that?" I snapped, trying to pull away, but he just held me tighter. "That doesn't make any—"

"It's in the journal, Cammie." Zach's gaze bore into mine. "It's all in the journal."

"Cammie!" someone said.

"I think I see her!" someone else called.

I could hear my classmates' voices in my ear. I knew they had crossed the fence and were running closer, but Zach's gaze never left mine.

"Look at me." Zach's hands felt like a vise. "Read the journal, Gallagher Girl. Read it all."

And then he pulled me closer, squeezed me so tightly that I could barely breathe. He pressed his lips hard against my forehead for a split second—nothing more—and when he finally let me go and disappeared back into the trees, I thought that I might fall.

"Oh my gosh, Cam, are you okay?" Eva Alvarez was screaming. "Are you—"

I heard Eva stop, breathless. I watched her pull up short and turn to stare with the rest of my classmates at the scene that lay behind me. The agents. The chaos. The blood. And the way our former teacher lay on his stomach in the middle of it all, hands bound, legs shackled. Unconscious.

"Is that Mr. Solomon?" Anna asked.

"Yes." Bex's voice was low.

"What . . ." Tina's voice caught. "What is that?"

"It was a trap."

Chapter twenty-eight

You may think that it would be impossible for a van full of teenage girls to be completely quiet for the duration of a two-hour drive, but that night I didn't hear a single voice. A soft rain fell, and only the sloshing of windshield wipers—the sound of water splashing against the undercarriage of the car—could break the stifling silence on the long ride back to school.

I recognized the sound. I'd heard it once in our Arlington town house as neighbors brought casseroles and condolences. I'd felt it at the ranch as relatives I barely knew spilled onto my grandparents' porch, the four walls of the house too thin to hold us and the news that my father was never coming home. The junior CoveOps class was mourning, and one by one, every girl in the van came to realize what my roommates and I had known for weeks—that Mr. Solomon hadn't been on a mission. Mr. Solomon was a whole different kind of gone.

When we pulled through the gates that night, it seemed like every light in the mansion was on. I could imagine girls inside, laughing and heading downstairs for supper, talking about papers and tests. But as we crawled from the van and watched Agent Townsend stride through the front doors, we all stayed perfectly still, a heavy drizzle and the memory of all we'd seen settling down around us, no one wanting to carry it all inside.

"I never knew," Anna Fetterman said. "I never even guessed. I'm making a mistake, aren't I?" She looked right at me as if I should know. "I shouldn't be on the CoveOps track. I shouldn't . . . I never knew."

"No one knew." Eva Alvarez placed an arm around Anna's shoulders. "No one knew what he was."

"*Is.*"

No one heard me whisper, but that was just as well. After all, no one else had stood in the amusement park graveyard and heard him say the Circle was coming. No one else had felt his warm hands on the bridge. I might have been the only Gallagher Girl in the world at that moment who knew that Mr. Solomon wasn't in the past tense.

So I walked toward the doors and stepped inside, certain of one thing: Joe Solomon was very much alive.

Well, actually, technically, I *tried* to step inside.

Girls filled the entryway and covered the stairs, and it took all the strength I could muster to press out of the rain and into the crowd that was staring as my mother and Agent Townsend stood in the middle of the foyer floor.

"What's going—"

"Shhh," a senior hissed, stopping Tina midsentence.

"You're welcome, by the way," Townsend said, turning toward the stairs, but my mother blocked him, looking anything but grateful.

"You had no right to take my daughter out of my school—"

"*Your* school?"

He should have been afraid. The last time I'd seen my mother look that way had been on a street in Washington, D.C., as her sister lay bleeding.

He should have been terrified.

"My daughter is not some pawn to be used on a whim!"

"Now, Rachel, don't think of her as a pawn. It's more like ... what is it you Americans say ... we dangled an apple out in front of Joe Solomon and—"

"The term is *carrot*," my mother corrected. "And it doesn't apply to teenage girls."

There was a knowing gleam in Townsend's eyes as he smiled. "Oh, is it? Maybe you use apples for something else."

Some people think the key to strength is knowing how to hit—how to shift your weight, time your blow, land the punch just right. But that's not it. As I stood peering through the crowd at my mother and the man who had taken me out of the safety of the mansion, I knew real strength is *not* hitting when what you want to do most is kill.

Townsend must have sensed it too, because something changed in him then. "We had thirty agents in the park's interior and another sixty on the perimeter grid. We had eyes on her the whole time. We knew Solomon would show himself, and as soon as he did, our agents were on him. She was fine."

He leaned closer to my mother, not blinking, not teasing, not even mocking. He laughed, but not like it was funny. It was closer to a laugh of disbelief.

"Ms. Morgan, we got him!"

"If you ever put a student at this school in danger again—"

"Oh, I thought you Gallagher Girls were immune to danger."

Despite the hundred girls that filled the foyer, no one moved or gasped or tried to defend our honor. We stood silently, waiting for our headmistress to say, "Oh, we are quite used to being underestimated, Agent Townsend. In fact, we welcome it."

That conversation probably violated every spy code and teacher code and headmistress code known to man, but that didn't matter. They couldn't see the hundred girls who stood watching. Despite their training, they didn't hear the way we held our collective breath. This fight was like the tide: it had been a long time coming and there was no way to hold it back.

"Joe Solomon agreed to take this job only when he knew he would be teaching your daughter, isn't that right."

Mom folded her hands in front of her. "I've already answered that question in great detail for people with far more authority than you."

"And that didn't strike you as odd? A man like Joe Solomon coming *here*?" He laughed again. "But of course the Circle has always liked to recruit agents young. What is it they say, the greener the fruit, the easier it turns?"

"Yes," my mother admitted.

"He was here a year and a half?" Townsend asked, but my mother's voice was calm, as if he'd asked about the weather.

"He was."

"That's a long time—long enough to recruit anyone he might need. Turn someone?"

"As I already informed your superiors, Agent Townsend, if the Circle has any allies here, they'd better pray that you find them before I do."

Agent Townsend was a large man, for covert operations. He was at least six inches taller and seventy pounds heavier than my mother (and that wasn't counting his ego), and yet there wasn't a doubt in my mind that he knew she was exactly right.

He watched her slowly turn and start up the stairs. She was almost gone when he called, "Joe Solomon isn't going to hurt your daughter, Ms. Morgan. You don't have to worry about him hurting anyone ever again."

I realized in that moment that he believed it—he really did—and for a second I wanted to believe *him*. He was a good spy, after all. A senior operative. A teacher. And standing there, surrounded by my sisterhood, I might have convinced myself that it was true—that I was safe.

But then my mother stopped and turned.

"I'm sorry, Agent Townsend, but Joe Solomon is the least of Cammie's worries."

Our chef was making my favorite soup for dinner, but my room-mates and I didn't run to the Grand Hall. We stood silently side by side while the rest of our school slowly drifted down the halls and up the stairs, carried away by a wave of gossip and fear and disbelief.

"Sublevel Two." I didn't whisper. I know that was foolish now, but at that moment, I, Cammie the Chameleon, didn't have the strength to hide. "We're *going* to find a way into Sub-level Two."

Chapter twenty-nine

How Not to Break Into
Sublevel Two
(A list by Cameron Morgan, with
help from Macey McHenry)

- **Digging:** Because a person would have to dig...
  a lot. And besides, the maintenance staff would
  totally notice any big holes that appeared in the
  middle of the lacrosse field. (Plus, it can totally ruin
  a manicure.)

- **Anything involving an elevator shaft:** Sure, every
  Gallagher Girl gets her very own crowbar on the first
  day of eighth grade, but it's not as simple as prying
  open the doors and shimmying on down to the subs.
  (Besides, in our experience, doors at the Gallagher
  Academy aren't exactly pry-able.)

- **Sweet-talk:** Because sweet-talking might make the sweet-talk*ee* suspicious about the sweet-talk*er*'s plans and motivations—not to mention that even the burliest members of the security staff are probably afraid of taking us into the sublevels and getting... you know...killed.

- **Teleportation:** Sure, Liz says she has an excellent working theory, but she doesn't have a prototype yet, and without a prototype it's pretty much a moot point.

- **That thing Bex's parents did in Dubai with liquid nitrogen, an earthquake simulator, and a ferret:** Because we don't have a ferret.

———

It only took three weeks.

I know that sounds like a lot of time—and it is. But also, it isn't. Because...well...in the clandestine services, nothing ever happens quickly (except when it does). Nothing is ever, ever easy (except when it is). And, most of all, nothing ever goes perfectly according to plan (except in the movies).

It's dirty work that is almost universally slow, tedious, repetitious, mundane, morose, and just in general boring (except for the parts when people might die).

We could have done it sooner and it still wouldn't have felt soon enough. We could have planned for years and we still wouldn't have felt ready. So, yeah. It took three weeks.

For Liz to crack the code. For Macey and Bex to gather the gear. For me to plan our way inside.

By one a.m. on the night in question, we were making our way down the third-floor corridor as quickly and as quietly as we could without making it obvious that we were trying to be both quick and quiet.

The Operatives fully understood that the first step in Denial and Deception Operations is denial. And it's way easier to deny being involved in some rogue, undercover operation if you're wearing jammies.

"There's something I still don't understand," Liz whispered. "If Mr. Solomon is so desperate to have this book or whatever it is that is located inside Sublevel Two, then why did he make it impossible to access Sublevel Two?"

"Because he wanted to make it impossible for the *wrong* people to access it," I said, peeking around the corner, where, as if on cue, Agent Townsend bounded down the stairs.

I threw myself against the wall, forgetting that we hadn't broken any rules at that point and there were at least a dozen perfectly valid reasons we might have been there. But I'm a chameleon. I'll take being invisible over being justifiable any day.

His footsteps echoed like thunder in the empty hallway.

I didn't watch him as I whispered, "It's time."

At 0135 hours, The Operatives proceeded to the small stairway beneath the Grand Stairs, but they didn't stop at the mirror that concealed the elevator to the sublevels.

At 0136, Operative Morgan's stomach began to growl, and the entire team realized the importance of not skipping meals prior to incredibly important covert operations!

Bex led us to the small closet at the base of the stairs and pulled out a backpack stocked with utility belts, cables, and a very handy gadget that Macey had made in her Intro to Accessories class (which is never about what new students think it's going to be about).

And as we stepped outside, I realized that it was warmer. Spring was coming, but I had barely noticed.

"Look." I stopped and looked at my three best friends in the whole world. "We've only got three minutes until the guards are going to patrol this sector, and I totally understand if you don't want to go. I don't know if this is going to work, and even if it does, we don't know exactly what we're going to face down there."

From the look on Bex's face, I knew there was no way she was going to be left out of anything this covert. And dangerous. And utterly gray in the black-and-white spectrum of right and wrong.

Still, I had to go on. "If anything ever happened to any of you..." I started, but then I couldn't finish.

"So if there's a computer down there that we've got to hack into in sixty seconds, you're going to do it?" Liz asked, strapping a belt on over her pajamas.

"And you really think I'm going to miss this?" Bex pulled her belt from the top of the pile.

We all looked at Macey. "You need me," she said, reaching for her belt like a queen taking her scepter.

As I leaned down and disabled the security devices around the small grate, I felt Bex watching over my shoulder.

"I always thought the elevators to Sublevel Two put us out somewhere over there." She pointed in the opposite direction.

I smiled up at her. "But we're not going to the elevators, are we?"

At precisely 0147, The Operatives tested their theory that the mirrors in the new compacts from McHenry Cosmetics are the appropriate size to slide over and deflect the laser beams that cover the opening of all ventilation points.

(The Operatives were correct.)

At precisely 0207, The Operatives tested the new Electromagnetic Signal Reallocator (Official Name and Patent Pending) that Operative Sutton had developed for the occasion.

(It was successful.)

At precisely 0208, Operative Baxter said a prayer. And jumped.

The airshaft was small. Crazy small. I'm-really-glad-I-skipped-dinner-after-all small. There was no way a grown man could have fit. It was an entrance that was only suitable for a girl. A Gallagher Girl, I thought as I slid down the cable like it was a fireman's pole, the clamp in my hand growing hot, searing into my gloves as I zoomed into the depths of the ground.

I knew Bex was below me, but I couldn't see a thing. Macey and Liz were above me, and I hoped that was why I couldn't see even the faintest hint of light above me as I hurtled into what felt like the world's tiniest volcano.

Deeper and deeper I went. Faster and faster I fell. I felt the air rushing past me, my hair blowing away from my face, the cable burning hotter in my hands until . . .

"Look out!" Bex yelled, as suddenly I broke free of the shaft. My arms felt as if they might pop out of their sockets when I squeezed the clamp and slammed to an almost instantaneous stop. I was dangling from the cable, looking down into the cavernous space of Sublevel Two.

"I can't believe that worked," I admitted, breathless.

"Cam!" Bex shouted, stopping me before I could release my hold on the cable. "Don't. Move. A muscle."

We were suspended thirty feet above the hard stone floor of a room that, despite a semester of studying in Sublevel Two, I'd never seen before. The subs are a vast and winding maze of classrooms and offices, resource libraries and storage for some of the covert world's most highly classified secrets. And right then, Bex and I were looking through the dim glow of security lights at a massive room filled with hundreds of shelves and filing cabinets, a complex system of wiring and explosives. . . .

And the most complex laser grid system I had ever seen.

"So," Bex said, smiling up at me through the pulsing glow of the emergency floodlamps, "wanna hang out?"

A moment later, the vibrations on the cable grew stronger, and I looked up in time to see Liz hurtling toward me through the air, stopping just above me.

Macey was close behind and out of breath as she asked, "What is all this?"

Bex and I looked down at the rows of top secret information and the high-grade explosives that ran the length of the room, neither of us able to hide the awe in our voices. "It's a burn bag," we said in unison.

"What's that?" Macey asked.

"It's the stuff that can't fall into the wrong hands. Ever. It's the stuff that's rigged to blow up in case . . . in case the worst happens."

Which was true. But scary. Because at that moment, technically, the worst that could happen was us.

Bex was the first to drop to the floor, nimble as a cat, landing between the red beams, then flipping and jumping through the air, navigating her way to the small panel on the side of the room. If it hadn't been so utterly terrifying, it would have been beautiful. Like ballet. But with a way higher casualty rate.

"Now, Liz," she yelled, and Liz pulled out her crossbow and took aim at the wall six inches above Bex's head.

"Uh . . . Liz . . ." Macey started.

"Sorry," Liz said, and raised her aim about a foot.

I don't think any of us could draw a breath as the arrow sailed through the air, a small cable trailing behind it, then landed perfectly just above the panel on the wall.

"Awesome," I said. "Now, just like we practiced—take the extra clip on your harness and put it on Bex's cable. Yeah. Just like that. You're doing—"

"Whoopsie daisy."

And that's when Elizabeth Sutton, supergenius, forgot that her bag was unzipped and let her Advanced Encryption textbook fall, end-over-end, into the heart of the laser field below.

"Liz!" I yelled, but it was too late. Lights began to pulse. Below us, the lasers began to move, red lines snaking over the ground, and I realized our only option.

"What do we do?" Macey yelled.

"We run!"

As we dropped to the ground, I couldn't hear my own thoughts—much less the footsteps of the girls who ran beside me. Red lights swirled. Sirens screamed. It was as if Sublevel Two were burning as Liz carried her laptop to where Bex stood waiting by the electronic nerve center that controlled all of Sublevel Two's modern defenses.

But modern . . . yeah, modern was the least of our problems.

At the far end of the room, there was a massive window made of stained glass. For a second I stood there, wondering why anyone would install a window in an underground room. It would have been far more weird and way less terrifying if the space behind the glass hadn't been quickly filling up with water.

"So that's coming from . . ." Macey started.

"The lake."

"So if we don't stop this..." she started again.

"We drown," I said, but Macey was already gone—sprinting across the room.

"What do we do?" she cried. She was searching the walls, pushing on stones—frantically looking for a way to make the water stop rising. "Where's the switch? I thought Mr. Solomon told Zach there was a way to turn it off."

As the water rose, the stained glass seemed to sparkle. The light looked different the higher the water went, and I couldn't help but remember the very first assignment Joe Solomon had ever given me: notice things.

"I've seen this before," I said, still staring at the familiar images in the glass—brightly colored shapes and lines. "Macey, have you seen it before?"

"Sorry, Cam," she said, still searching. "I'm a little busy here."

"It's like the one upstairs. You know, the big one? Except... different. It's almost like..." I trailed off. My voice caught. And I knew what we had to do. "It's not a window—it's a puzzle!"

The glass was cold to the touch when I reached for it. The device was at least a hundred years old, and when I pushed on a deep blue section of glass, at first it didn't budge, and I thought I was wrong. But I pushed harder and... movement. The window was like a kaleidoscope, a moving, swirling mass of glass and hidden gears as I slid the blue section smoothly into place in the center of the massive frame.

"Macey, help me," I said, and together we went to work, our

eyes and hands feverishly flying over the window's hundreds of sections as quickly and deftly as we could, trying to duplicate the upstairs window that I had never truly looked at until Joe Solomon came to our school.

All around us, though, the sirens kept blaring. The lights kept swirling. And, worst of all, the water kept rising.

"Lizzie?" I heard Bex yell behind me.

"Almost . . ." Liz said, her fingers flying over the laptop's keys. "Almost . . . *got it*!"

Instantly, the sirens went silent. The lights stopped swirling. From the corner of my eye, I saw Liz and Bex give each other a high five, but the water level kept rising.

I thought of what Mr. Mosckowitz had told Agent Townsend that night in the shadowy halls—that every generation had added a layer of defense to that honored place—and I knew that the original Gallagher Girls were in many ways the wisest.

"Got it!" Macey yelled, pushing the final piece into place, but nothing happened.

It felt like an eternity before a shrill mechanical voice sounded through the echoing space. "IDENTIFY. IDENTIFY. IDENTIFY. WHO GOES THERE?" it asked.

And then instinct must have taken hold, because the four of us shouted the first words that came to mind: "We are the sisters of Gillian!"

I held my breath and said a prayer until the water began to recede and the mechanical voice said, "WELCOME HOME."

Chapter thirty

There are things people like Townsend would never understand about the Gallagher Academy. Ever. You see, it isn't about being a Gallagher Girl—it's about being *one* of the Gallagher Girls. Plural. All of us. Without Bex, I would have triggered the sensors. Without Macey, I might never have solved the puzzle in time. And without Liz . . . well, Liz had multiple roles on this particular mission.

"How high is that again?" she said as she walked beside me.

"Not *that* high," I said slowly, looking up at the towering shelves that lined the walls of Sublevel Two.

It wasn't where we stored the chemicals. As I looked around the long rows of tall shelves, there wasn't a single weapon in sight. But the information contained within this room was volatile enough to bring my school crashing down, potent enough to poison every member of our sisterhood. And I knew we didn't dare stay too long—that we live our lives on a need-to-know basis for a reason.

Unfortunately, I was the only one who felt that way.

"Ooh! Cool!" I heard Macey cry from one row away, despite the fact that, upstairs, half of the Gallagher Academy security team was now on high alert, wondering what in the world had just happened in Sublevel Two.

"Hey, Cam," Bex called, "did you know Amelia Earhart spent the last twenty years of her life undercover in Istanbul?"

A half second later, Macey came running around the end of an aisle, a file in her hands. "Quick, guys, I've got pictures of Professor Buckingham . . . in World War Two . . . in a swimsuit!"

Bex raced to look at the images, but my gaze was locked on Liz as I ran a cable through the utility belt that hung around her tiny waist.

"Liz, this is silly. I'll do it," I told her.

"But Cammie, Zach said it's in the very middle of the highest shelf. It's going to be really hard to get someone in exactly the right place, and I'm the lightest," she said, citing the one scientifically verifiable—and thus relevant—piece of information we had.

"You don't have to prove anything, Lizzie. I can—"

"They need you, Cammie," she said, her voice no louder than a whisper. "And if their side needs you alive . . . our side needs you alive." She looked up at the tall shelves and took a deep breath as if clearing all those unpleasant thoughts away and focusing on a single, quantifiable fact: "I'm the lightest."

"Bex, we're ready," I called out. A second later she appeared, Liz's crossbow in her hands. It looked absolutely effortless as she took aim at the ceiling fifty feet overhead. I heard a cable whirling, watched the coil at my feet slowly disappear, until I heard the metallic noise that titanium makes when it strikes solid stone.

"Ready?" I asked Liz, who nodded.

"You can do it," I silently whispered while Bex grasped the other end of the cable and pulled. In the next moment, Liz was floating gracefully (or as gracefully as Liz does anything) over the shelves marked: WARNING, HIGH VOLTAGE.

I stood, holding my breath as I watched. Maybe that's why I was the one who heard it, a buzzing sound, so distant that at first I thought it was the whirling of my own mind.

But then I heard it again.

"Did you guys hear that?" I asked, straining.

Bex was trying to maneuver Liz into position, and Liz was staring at the high-voltage sign as if her life depended on it, which ... well ... it probably did.

"Do you hear that?" I asked Macey.

"We're five hundred yards beneath the ground," she said with a shrug.

She was right, of course. I was probably as safe here as I could have possibly been anywhere in the world, but there was something about the eerie quiet that surrounded us. I stood for a long time, listening to the sound of my heartbeat—a rhythm that hadn't slowed in months until ...

"There," I said again, and this time Macey stopped too.

"Maybe it's a furnace or something?" she asked as the sound got louder.

I held my breath. "That's no heating unit."

"How much longer, Liz?" Bex asked.

"Almost got it!" she called, reaching as far as her thin frame would go, but still the book stayed out of grasp.

"Liz," I said again. The noise was growing louder, and it came with more regularity. "Liz, how long would it take you to bring the laser grid back up?"

"Two minutes," she said.

But in the depths of the space, the noise growled to life again. I looked at Bex and Macey. "We don't have two minutes."

In that moment there were a lot of fears that came to mind:

What if there was some backup security measure that we hadn't neutralized and we were about to be gassed, crushed, drowned, electrocuted, pinned, or trapped?

What if the Circle had tracked me into the depths of our school and, knowing that I was locked away from my mother and our guards, had found a way inside?

What if it was my mother, and we were caught . . . busted?

But despite my crazy fears, there was one thing I knew for certain: someone else was trying to get into Sublevel Two.

"You can do it, Lizzie," Bex shouted up. "Just . . . hurry. And maybe move a little to the—"

Bex pulled the rope to the right, but either she underestimated her own strength or overestimated Liz's weight, because next I saw a blond blur swing past the shelves and stop to hover somewhere over the section dedicated to the Cuban Missile Crisis.

The mechanic whirring had grown louder, and now we could tell it was coming from somewhere in front of us.

"Are those..." Macey started.

"The elevator shafts?" Bex guessed.

"I think so," I said. "Do you think it's—"

"Townsend," we all said in unison.

"But how is he planning on getting around the security measures down here?" Macey asked.

I shrugged. "Either he knows we've already done it for him..."

"Or he doesn't care," Bex said, staring at me, and I could tell from the look in her eyes that neither of us knew which was scarier.

A small pile of dust had started to appear on the floor, and I noticed the small hole that was appearing in the stone wall. Agent Townsend was drilling his way out of the shaft and into Sublevel Two.

I spoke over the sound of the drill and the panic of my pounding heart. "We gotta go!"

The Operatives realized they were about to have a very hostile encounter with a very angry teacher-slash-possible-enemy-agent, so they utilized a number of highly recommended covert tactics.

1. Operative McHenry said, "Are you ready yet? Are you ready yet? Are you ready yet?" in rapid succession until Operative Sutton was, in fact, ready.

2. Operative Morgan pushed a shelf in front of the wall the enemy operative was trying to drill through, forming a temporary barricade.

3. Operative Baxter took that opportunity to say some very choice words about the Gallagher Academy's new Covert Operations instructor.

"Got it!" Liz said, and in the next second she was sailing through the air, falling. Macey and I caught her and guided her to the ground, but we barely had a second to unhook her—not a moment to retrieve any of our gear—before Bex grabbed my arm and whispered, "Run!"

And then we were off, dodging through the shelves as quickly and quietly as we possibly could.

Glancing back, I could see the beam of a flashlight playing over the shelves at the end of the massive room. We were well away from the beam's reach, but we were anything but safe.

The cable still dangled from the ventilation shaft in front of us. I watched Macey grip hold of it, latch on to one of the clamps that had brought us down, and shift the device into reverse. A split second later, she was rising through the air, hurtling into the shaft, toward the night sky and freedom.

But in Sublevel Two there were footsteps behind us and coming closer.

He's never been here before, I told myself as I listened to the man make his way slowly through the maze of shelves.

Bex was standing at the base of the cable, hurriedly securing Liz to the device, while I stayed frozen, watching the play of the flashlight between the shelves. It was eerie and beautiful at the same time. A hundred years' worth of covert items lay inside that massive space—blueprints and plans, secrets so explosive the best spies in the world were willing to risk everything to make sure they never saw the light of day.

But right then, there was only one top secret artifact that mattered to me. It was my turn, so I reached for the cable and felt myself rising faster and faster toward the fresh air of the night.

Chapter thirty-one

It was a nearly starless sky. Black clouds hung heavy overhead, blocking out the moon. But after the darkness of the tiny hole, I had to squint my eyes. It was like staring at the sun.

"And just when we thought we weren't going to get to do any CoveOps training exercises this semester," I said to Bex as she yanked me out of the hole by my arms; but my roommates weren't smiling.

"What?" I asked. My friends just looked at me. "What?" I asked again, but I never got to hear the answer, because in the next moment the air around us was drowned in light. Sirens were ringing, piercing the air, screaming that something was terribly, terribly wrong.

The front doors of the mansion were a hundred yards away, but I knew they were our best chance at safety, and Bex and Liz were already running. Macey and I hurried to catch up.

Guards ran from the main mansion to the fences, checking

the perimeter, barely able to restrain barking dogs on the ends of long leashes.

Searchlights flashed across the sky. From a distance, it might have looked like a party. People in Roseville probably had a dozen crazy theories about what was going on at the school right then, but none of them, I knew, would remotely resemble the truth.

The instant my roommates and I pushed breathlessly through the front doors, I heard Professor Buckingham call my name from the top of the stairs.

"Cameron Morgan! Has anyone seen Cameron—"

"There she is!" an eighth grader yelled, and in the next second I was trapped in a crush of bodies. Mr. Smith reached me first. A man from the security department grabbed me from the other side.

"What's happening?" I asked, looking at Mr. Smith.

"Breach," he said simply as I was dragged (or practically carried) up the stairs.

Girls crowded the hallways. They had pajamas and bare feet. And weapons. Oh yeah, they'd brought a lot of weapons.

"Is it the Circle?" one seventh grader yelled, voice breaking. "Are they here?"

But the faculty kept me gripped in a tight circle. I could barely make out a single face until Tina Walters broke through. "Cammie, are you okay?"

"I'm fine!" I yelled, trying to squirm free.

And then the alarms stopped.

"You gave us quite a scare tonight, young lady," Townsend greeted me on the landing. My friends stood at the bottom of the stairs, staring up at me. Their hair was tangled and full of cobwebs. Their faces were filthy (which meant mine probably was too). "Exactly where have you girls been keeping yourselves?"

"Secret passageway," I said. "I just found it. It's awesome but..." I glanced at Macey, who had a large black mark on one perfect cheekbone. "Dirty."

"You," Townsend said, pointing at Liz. "What do you have in that bag?"

Okay, so maybe it *did* look a little strange. After all, a hundred girls had filled the hallways and lined the staircases that night. There were face masks and retainers, but Liz carried the only backpack, and Townsend wouldn't have been the spy everyone thought he was if he hadn't wondered what was inside it.

"Well?" he asked again, stepping closer.

"Homework!" Liz blurted. "Books."

"You may not know this, Agent Townsend," Dr. Fibs said, "but Ms. Sutton here is one of our most dedicated—"

"Open it," Townsend demanded. He grabbed the bag and turned it upside down. I held my breath and watched as two notebooks, a pack of gum, and fourteen colored pencils scattered across the floor.

I'm pretty sure I was supposed to breathe a sigh of relief, but instead I felt panic. Terror. We'd risked our lives to get that journal, and it was nowhere. Gone.

"Where's the..." I found myself saying aloud, but Macey gave the slightest of nods. The journal was hidden, it told me. The journal was safe.

"Cammie!"

I knew that voice.

"Mom," I said, trying to see through the crowd.

"It's okay, everyone," my mother—our headmistress—told us. "The security department assures me that the perimeter has not been breached. There's no one within the mansion or the grounds who is not supposed to be here. Go back to bed, everybody." When she looked at me, there was no doubt it was an order. "Go *straight* to bed."

Yeah. In case you're wondering, we totally didn't do that.

Sure, we went to our suite. Sure, we turned out the lights. But ten seconds later the four of us were huddled in the bathroom, staring at the book that looked especially dark in Liz's pale hand. When she handed it to me, a single piece of paper slipped free, fluttered, and landed on the floor.

Dear Cammie,

If you're reading this, I must be gone. I know I should probably apologize for keeping this journal from you for so long, but I won't, because I'm not sorry. In my professional opinion, you weren't ready. And in my personal opinion, I had hoped you never would be.

I've made mistakes, Cammie—too many to name

here. But the biggest of which, I still carry. The worst of which, I've spent a lifetime trying to make right.

I did try to make it right, Cammie. I really tried, but if you're reading this, I must not have tried quite hard enough.

Forever sorry,

Joseph Solomon

The thin book felt heavier then, more precious than all of the first editions in the Gallagher Academy's library put together. The cover was brittle and dry. The pages yellow with age. I was almost afraid to open it. But needless to say, *not* reading it wasn't really a viable option at that point.

I took a deep breath and turned to the first page, read the heading—COVERT OPERATIONS REPORT—but beyond that, I couldn't read a single word.

"It's encrypted," Bex hissed in frustration. "We risked our bloody necks and we can't even read it. I tell you, I'm half tempted to break into CIA custody just so I can break Joe Solomon out of CIA custody just so I can break Joe Solomon."

But at the word *encrypted*, Liz had snatched the journal from my hands and was holding it up to the light.

"It's the pigeons!" she shouted, and I worried that Tina, Eva, Courtney, and the rest of the junior class might come barging into our suite with crossbows and curling irons.

"This is it," Liz said, jabbing her finger onto the page. "See, look at this. It's almost more like hieroglyphs in a way. Almost like a—"

"Language," Macey said.

Liz's eyes shone in the dim room. "Yeah, that's exactly it."

"And you don't crack languages—not really," Bex said. "You learn them."

"Or you translate them," Macey said.

"Exactly. Mr. Solomon didn't leave a bunch of crazy scribblings on a board. . . ." Liz started.

"He left a key." Macey reached out to take the book. She ran her finger over the page. "Is this Mr. Solomon's handwriting?"

"No," I heard myself whisper. "It's my dad's."

Chapter thirty-two

Covert Operations Report

(Translation by Operatives Morgan and Sutton)

Day 1
Joe's nightmares are back.

He says they're nothing, but I can hear him screaming down the hall—something about Blackthorne and Vatican City. Last night I ran to his room and found him reaching, half asleep, for a knife.

He says he had an op go bad there. Only problem is, according to Langley, Agent Joseph Solomon has never been to Rome.

Day 26
I wish someone would tell me that it's okay to spy on my best friend. I keep this journal in code. I listen to

his calls. Tonight I followed him to a dead letter drop in Georgetown.

I wish someone would tell me that I'm crazy. It would be far better than being right, because all I can think about is the passport I found in his safety deposit box (yeah, I also broke into his safety deposit box).

Three years ago he went to Rome on a passport not issued by the CIA—at the same time that someone tried to kill the Pope.

With a knife.

I really hope I'm crazy.

Day 92

I think I know what Joe was. What he is?

But...no. It can't be true.

I don't want it to be true.

Day 96

Some people say the Circle doesn't exist—that there is no ancient association of spies and assassins out to manipulate the world order, but it turns out they are real.

Turns out my roommate is one.

Turns out a lot of people are.

Day 100

Joe told me the truth tonight. Joe told me everything.

We're going to stop them. It might be the last thing we ever do, but we'll do it.

I didn't dare linger on those last words—think about what they meant.

"How old were they when they wrote that?" Bex asked.

I looked at the date at the corner of the page and did the math in my head. "Twenty-three," I said, and then I *re-did* the math, because it didn't seem right that my father had started chasing the Circle of Cavan before he'd even started dating my mother—that this mission was officially older than I was.

"*Turn*," Liz said, not trying to hide her impatience at being forced to read at a non-speed-of-light pace, but these were the last things my father would ever say to me. I wanted to make every sentence count.

Day 219
After nine months of bureaucracy and protocol, Operatives Morgan and Solomon have concluded that the criminal organization known as the Circle of Cavan has too many double agents placed within official intelligence organizations to be effectively neutralized through official channels.

It's a good thing Operatives Morgan and Solomon are very good at being unofficial.

Day 290
After two weeks in Rome, The Operatives have ascertained that the Circle's base of operations here

has been shut down or relocated since Operative Solomon was sent to the Vatican.

They have also learned that a person will really get sick of pasta. Eventually.

Day 407

Today, Hungarian officials positively identified the body of the man found in a river in Budapest as the man who was thinking of providing intel to The Operatives about the Circle's Eastern European operations.

They killed him.

He was the best lead we've had in over a year, and they killed him.

The air around us was warmer; it was almost spring; and yet there were goose bumps on our arms. It still felt a long, long way from summer.

Day 506

The Deputy Director warned The Operatives again about taking on the Circle themselves, but Operative Solomon insists that the Circle has recruited too long and too well to be effectively targeted by a large-scale operation.

The Circle has spies. Literally. The Circle has spies everywhere.

The Operatives must go on alone.

The more I read, the faster I turned the pages until, finally, I flipped to the end, desperate to read the last page first—as if, maybe, this time it might have a different ending.

Day 5,860
The Operatives received word that their asset in Athens has had a breakthrough. Operative Solomon has begun preparations to travel to Greece, but the Deputy Director of the CIA suspects The Operatives are still taking on the Circle on their own, so he has placed Operative Solomon on desk duty. Operative Morgan will go instead.

My father was thirty-nine when he wrote that, and the book was almost out of pages—the story, in a lot of ways, was almost at its end. So I held my breath and turned the page and saw that the handwriting had changed. My father's lazy scrawl was gone—replaced with the precise penmanship that I'd seen scribbled across the sublevel blackboards for the past year and a half.

Day 5,869
Cutout made contact today with word that Operative Morgan did not appear at their meeting. Cutout will follow backup protocols again until Operative Morgan shows.

Day 5,878

Operative Solomon arrived at Operative Morgan's safe house in Athens, but it appears he never made it this far. Will begin backtracking immediately.

Day 5,892

CIA has been contacted. Full force of The Agency is now involved in the search for Operative Morgan.

Day 5,900

Three weeks of looking and the trail has gone cold.

    He's gone.

    He's just gone.

    Someone has to tell Rachel.

Chapter THIRTY-THREE

THINGS THAT WOULD NEVER BE
THE SAME, NEVER, EVER AGAIN
(A list by Cameron Morgan)

- Macey's pajama pants: because grass stains and air shaft dirt never come out.

- Agent Townsend's reputation: because if word ever got out that the four of us had done what he'd been trying to do for months, I'm pretty sure they'd take away his double-0 status (if Tina was even right that he had one).

- Liz: because the Pigeon Code had opened up a whole new world of cryptography (and she was already pretty obsessed with the old one).

- Bex: because her parents had been right.

- Bex: because her parents had been wrong.

- Me: just because.

————

The next night I walked toward my mother's office carrying my father's journal and my teacher's secret. I had no idea which one was heavier.

"It wasn't Sodium Pentothal, was it?"

I spun at the sound and saw Agent Townsend standing in the Hall of History, staring at me through the protective glow of Gilly's—I mean Cavan's—sword.

"In the apple?" he clarified.

"I don't know what you're—" I tried to push past him and into my mother's office, but his hand was on my arm. His breath was warm in my ear.

"You can try to lie to me, but I wouldn't recommend it."

My father's journal was in my backpack, and it felt like a talisman, giving me strength. "Get your hand off of me." Townsend eyed me but didn't move, and I tried to twist free. "Teachers can't manhandle students and make wild accusations. The trustees would never—"

"Oh, but the trustees have been employing a famous double agent for almost two years. They're very eager to help."

"I'm still a student at this school and—"

"Now, now, Ms. Morgan. Either you're a trained operative I'm supposed to distrust and respect, or a sixteen-year-old girl—"

"Just turned seventeen," I corrected him.

"—I'm supposed to go easy on. You can't have it both ways." He released my arm and stepped away. "I would have thought your precious Mr. Solomon would have taught you better than that."

"He's not *my* Mr. Solomon."

"Sure he is. Isn't that why you and your little friends tried to hack into my records? Stake out my office? Put some nasty concoction inside the apple of an unsuspecting teacher?"

I didn't say a thing.

"That's good; don't deny it. Denying the undeniable just makes you sound like a fool as well as a liar. In this profession, you can be one—sometimes the other. But never both."

He moved through the Hall of History, eyeing our most prized possessions as if they were trinkets at a fair.

He didn't face me as he asked, "You believed him, didn't you? Thought he was a good guy? Well, that's your mistake. No one—and I do mean no one—in this line of work is ever a truly good guy. If we were, we'd be doing something bloody well different from this."

He didn't know what he was talking about. He didn't know…anything. I started toward my mother's office, needing her more than ever, desperate to show her—to prove that we weren't fools.

"She's not in there," he called across the empty hall. I felt my blood turn cold.

"Where is she?"

He smiled slightly. "Gone."

191

"What did you do to her?"

"Me?" He laughed. Yes, actual *laughage*. "Allow me to clear some things up for you, Ms. Morgan." He stepped closer. "I'm not a member of the Circle. I've never even *seen* Blackthorne. Of course, we probably had something like it—wouldn't rule it out." He shook his head. "But I was never a part of that."

"A part of what?"

"I *am* the bloody good guy."

I stood silent, watching him walk away, until . . .

"You're wrong!" I yelled, the words echoing down the empty hall. "You're wrong about everything!"

Agent Townsend stopped and turned slowly.

"Nine hours ago, a CIA transport team was ambushed outside of Langley. Three guards were killed and Joe Solomon was taken." He stared at me down the long corridor. "Your *innocent man* is back with the Circle tonight, Ms. Morgan. They have him. He's free."

That night I had the strangest dream. I was standing at the top of the Grand Staircase in a long beautiful dress. I heard the sounds of the Virginia reel come sweeping toward me, and below me, people crowded the foyer floor. But the strangest thing of all was that my father was standing at the bottom of the staircase, waiting.

I descended the stairs and took his arm, and together we made our way through the crowd that filled the Grand Hall. There was dancing and drinking. It was a party, but the feeling in the room was that there was no reason at all to celebrate.

And then suddenly, a man appeared, holding a sword.

I knew I had to stop him—I had to make it stop—but the man moved faster toward where I stood. His eyes pulled closer in the dim ballroom, and I stared at a face I know.

A face I've kissed.

"No." I might have said the word, but a hand was over my mouth. Strong arms were holding me down while I kicked at the covers wrapped tightly around my legs.

Then I heard a deep voice whisper my name. "Cammie, wake up."

"No," I mumbled, still fighting and half asleep.

"It's okay, Gallagher Girl. It's okay. Wake up."

Chapter THIRTY-FOUR

There are many ways a self-respecting (not to mention *sane*) teenage girl might react to having a teenage boy suddenly appear in her bedroom in the middle of the night.

Hit.

Panic.

Flail.

Freeze.

But I didn't do any of them. Not right then, because I was lying tangled in the sheets and Zach's arms. Tears streamed down my face as I thought of my father and Mr. Solomon and Gilly—for a split second I knew what it felt like to be Gilly.

"It's okay, Gallagher Girl." He smoothed my hair. "It was just a bad—"

"What are you doing here?" I whispered.

Two feet away, Liz shivered and rolled over. In the corner, Bex was starting to snore. Macey lay perfectly still on her back, her dark hair splayed across her pillow like Sleeping Beauty. I jerked my head in their direction.

"Tell me why I shouldn't wake them?" I whispered. "Tell me why I shouldn't push that?" I pointed to the panic button on the wall.

He smiled. "Now, where would be the fun in that?"

"Zach," I hissed, and let my hand creep closer to the button.

"Okay," he said, reaching out to gently take that very hand. "I'm here because we need to take a walk."

When we were in the tenth grade, Zach went to my school for an entire semester. We'd shared the halls as classmates. As equals. But walking into Madame Dabney's empty tearoom, the playful look he'd had in his eyes that semester was completely gone. I'm not sure what kind of look I had in my eyes, because I was totally avoiding my own reflection in the gilt-framed mirrors. (Now was *not* the time to be worried about pillow-cheek wrinkles and middle-of-the-night crazy hair.) Instead, I studied him.

"Do I *want* to know how you got in here?" I asked.

He shook his head. "I only broke a few laws." He held his fingers a half inch apart. "Little ones."

Dim chandeliers hung from an ornate ceiling. Our feet were quiet against the polished parquet floors. Almost a year ago we'd stood in this very spot while Madame Dabney ordered us to dance, but Zach didn't reach for me this time. I didn't feel like swaying anymore.

"Does the Circle really have him?" I asked.

"Yes." Zach's voice was flat as he ran his hand through his hair and dropped onto one of Madame Dabney's silk-covered fainting couches. He looked entirely out of place.

"Why? I mean, if he isn't working with them—"

"They weren't exactly doing him a favor. A cozy little CIA prison is probably looking pretty good to him about now."

I walked to the tall windows and stared out over the grounds. Zach's reflection stared back at me in the dark windows. Somehow it was easier not to face him.

"People don't leave the Circle easily, Gallagher Girl."

"I know."

"Anyone who knows how they work or where they work —anyone who knows anything . . ." As he trailed off, there was something new in his voice. He sounded tired in a way that had nothing to do with the hour.

"I know."

"They're tying up loose ends."

I tried to focus my eyes on the forest outside, the way the sun was just starting to color the sky. "Is that what I am?"

Zach stood and moved to my side at the window. Tears stung my eyes, and I kept my gaze on anything but him.

"Gallagher Girl," he said softly, reaching for me. "I don't know. But I promise we will find out."

A feeling swept through me when I thought back on the last year: Zach on a train racing through the Pennsylvania countryside; Zach lying beneath the bleachers in Ohio. And finally

Zach gripping my hand, leading me away from a white van on a dark street in Washington, D.C. Zach standing between me and an attacker's gun, the attacker looking at the boy beside me and saying, "You?"

"You should be dead, Zach." I looked down and saw the way my shadow stretched across the floor between us. "That night—in D.C.—he had a clear shot. *I* should be gone and *you* should be dead."

"Gallagher Girl . . ."

"Why didn't he shoot you?"

"Everything that night happened so fast, Gallagher Girl."

"My name is Cammie!" I didn't think about all the people I could have woken, all the alarms that might have gone off. I just snapped, "How did you know about Boston? Why are you working with Mr. Solomon now? Are you my friend or are you my enemy, Zach? Or, wait, let me guess, you can't tell me."

"I don't know why they want you. And for the rest . . . it's better if you don't know."

Need-to-know basis is a real thing. It exists for real reasons. But that doesn't mean I have to like it—and, coming from Zach, it sounded a whole lot different than it did coming from my mother.

"Why do *you* get to know?"

"What's the matter, Gallagher Girl? Jealous?"

"Yeah," I yelled, even though I'm pretty sure he'd been kidding. "I am."

"Cammie—"

"Time's up, Zach," I said. "Tell me what you know or—"

"Or what?" He reached for me. "You're not going to hurt me."

"I won't," I said, then risked a glance toward the door at the three angriest Gallagher Girls I had ever seen. "But *they* might."

Chapter tHiRtY-fivE

PROS AND CONS OF HAVING REALLY CUTE
BOYS SNEAK INTO YOUR SCHOOL TO SEE YOU

CON: It's a little creepy.

PRO: When someone else sneaks *in*, you get a lot more
sleep than when you have to sneak *out*.

CON: Impromptu visits by boys significantly increase the
chance that they'll see you in your least cute pajamas.

PRO: Almost everyone looks good in moonlight.

CON: Five hours of very deep sleep is almost guaranteed
to do very unfortunate things to your hair.

PRO: Waking up in the middle of the night means . . . well
. . . waking up.

CON: Eventually, whether you like it or not, your roommates are going to find out about it.

———

"Hello, Zachary," Macey said, striding in. "You're looking well."

"Hey, Macey." Zach turned to the shortest and blondest of us and tipped an imaginary hat. "Liz." And then finally, he looked back at Bex. "Rebecca."

If the use of Bex's full name was supposed to make her angry, it was entirely too late. She stood by the door, leaning against the frame with her arms crossed. Someone who didn't know her might have thought she was still tired, but I knew better. She was guarding the exit.

"We were talking about Mr. Solomon," I said.

Macey raised her eyebrows. "Oh, is *that* what you were doing?"

Bex kept her eyes on Zach. "What have you heard?" she asked.

Zach shook his head. "Not much more than you have. The Circle broke him out. The CIA is saying it's because he's with the Circle, but really—"

"It's because he's *against* them," Bex finished.

Zach nodded. "In almost two hundred years no one has come closer to bringing down the Circle than Mr. Solomon." Zach cut his eyes at me. "And your dad." He waited, as if I might burst into tears or something, but I didn't. "The Circle needs to know what Joe knows, and what he's told others."

"Like me?" I guessed.

Zach nodded slowly. "I'm willing to bet they're going to have a lot of questions about you."

"Good," Bex said. "That means they'll keep him alive."

I turned back to the window, stood staring out at the shadowy grounds. *They need him alive.*

"We're going to get him back. We *have* to get him back." I felt my roommates looking at me like I was crazy, but I turned to Zach. "Where would they take him?"

"I don't know."

"Don't lie to me, Zach. Don't tell me you don't know things, because you do. Now where would they take him?"

"I don't know! Do you think I'd be *here* if I knew?"

I've seen Zach in a lot of lights, but in the early morning haze, I saw him as he really was: a scared, parentless boy with absolutely no place to turn.

"What about the man the CIA has in custody—the one who shot Abby?" Macey asked. "He might know."

But Bex was shaking her head. "He's compromised. No way the Circle's still using anything he ever knew about."

"So that's just . . . it?" Liz asked. I could see it weighing on her. There were no databases to crack, no satellites to hack into. I thought about Mr. Solomon and his insistence that technology is a crutch, and a real spy should always be able to walk without it.

"Mr. Solomon would know," I admitted softly. "I wish we could ask him."

The room was quiet in the gray light of early morning. The school still slept. No one was jogging across the grounds. We were alone when Zach whispered, "Maybe we can."

* * *

"What do you mean there is a second journal?" Bex asked ten minutes later. She was looking at Zach, and Zach was looking *afraid*.

"The one Mr. Solomon hid in Sublevel Two was your dad's, Cammie. If anything ever happened . . . it was supposed to go to you. It was your dad's, so now it's *yours*. But Joe kept one too. It goes all the way back to his time with the Circle—all the way back to Blackthorne."

Zach stood at the windows, squinting against the slowly rising sun.

"No one has ever known more about the Circle than Joe. He started writing everything down as soon as they recruited him. And then when he realized what they were, he kept writing because . . . well . . . he knew something like this would happen eventually. He said if I ever needed it, I should go get it."

"Go where?" Macy asked.

Zach looked at the four of us for a long time before taking a deep breath. "Blackthorne."

I know it will sound crazy. I know you won't believe me. But in that split second I ran through every scenario I knew —calculated all the odds. It was an informed decision that made me say, "We'll go get it—right now. Before everyone is up. We'll—"

"We?" Bex cut me off. "You think *we* should . . . what? Jump into Liz's van, drive all night, break into a top secret facility, and, oh yeah, take you away from the safest place in the world?"

"Think about this, Cam," Liz said. "We don't have to go

anywhere. All we have to do is tell your mom, and she'll call the CIA and—"

"My mom's not here, remember? And you read Dad's reports —you know the Circle has people at every level of the CIA. Mr. Solomon knew he couldn't trust just anyone with this, and neither can we."

Bex shook her head. "No. It's too risky."

"It's not *that* risky. We drive up, get the journal, and see if it has any clues about where Mr. Solomon is. It's not like we're going to break him out by ours—"

"*What?*" Bex and I snapped at the exact same time, turning to stare at Zach, who was giving us the oddest look.

"Nothing." He crossed his arms and shrugged. "I was just wondering when the two of you switched bodies is all."

It was true. Bex was not supposed to be the cautious one, the careful one. But then again, a lot of things had changed on that bridge.

"I have to do this for him, Bex. I have to do *something*."

The sun was coming up over Roseville. I'd never seen it from that window, but it was especially beautiful with the early morning rays reflected in Madame Dabney's finest crystal. In that moment and that place, almost anything seemed to lie within our grasp. And maybe that's why Bex smiled. "Well, I have always wanted to see Blackthorne."

I looked at Liz. "I just tweaked the van to incorporate solar technology. It really needs a road test for statistical significance, you know."

"Us versus Blackthorne?" Macey said with a smile. "Yeah, I'm all for that."

I don't know how to explain it, but right then, things seemed okay. Our mission was clear.

We could go to Blackthorne.

We could get the journal.

Then we could find a way to bring Joe Solomon home.

Yes, in that moment everything was okay. But, of course, that moment could not last.

I remember the sound of the door as it swung open, the shocked, surprised look that crossed each of my roommates' faces as we turned to see the slim, dark silhouette that stood in the open doorway and said, "So when do we leave?"

My mother took two steps forward, then turned to stare at Zach. "Didn't I tell you to stay in my office?"

Chapter thirty-six

THINGS THAT REALLY, REALLY SURPRISED ME
ABOUT THAT PARTICULAR ROAD TRIP:

1. That it happened. At all.

2. That it happened *with a boy.*

3. That of all the people in the van, Bex spent the most time driving.

4. That after a whole day in a vehicle with nothing else to snack on, a person really can get sick of Peanut M&M's.

5. That even while sleeping in a van, Macey McHenry's hair never gets messed up.

6. That no one mentioned Mr. Solomon's name, not even once.

7. That no one talked about where we were going.

8. That four Gallagher Girls were playing hooky and missing an entire day of class (even *with* our headmistress's permission).

9. That, if you drive all night and only stop for essentials, the Blackthorne Institute for Boys is only ten hours away from the Gallagher Academy.

Somehow it had always felt much farther.

———

"Are you still mad at me?" Zach whispered as we crossed the Pennsylvania border. His leg was pressing against mine, but I didn't think about how it felt, because my mother (*who is a spy*) was riding shotgun in the front seat, and my roommates (*who are future spies*) were surrounding us in the van. And besides, it doesn't take a lot of training to know that leg-pressing can seriously divert a girl from little things, like trying not to die.

So I didn't say a word.

"Ooh," Zach whispered. "The silent treatment."

"I'm not talking to you, Zach," I whispered, whirling on him, "because I know you're not going to really *say* anything anyway. Should I be asking you more questions you refuse to answer?"

As I turned and faced forward again, watched the yellow lines of the highway flying by, I expected more excuses. More lies. But instead, Zach just leaned across me and whispered to Liz, "She's cute when she's silent."

I didn't utter a single word.

Not when he ate the last of the M&M's.

Not when he put his head on my shoulder and tried to take a nap.

Not when he and Liz thumb wrestled (despite the fact that I was sitting between them) for the better part of the state of Pennsylvania.

Not when Liz and Macey finally fell asleep and he leaned close to me and whispered, "Are you sure you wanna do this, Gallagher Girl?"

Nope. Not even then. I didn't have anything else to say.

At dusk, the silence broke as I heard my mother say, "Pull over here."

Bex pulled into the parking lot of an old gas station by the side of a narrow two-lane highway. Weeds grew up between abandoned pumps. Rusty machines bore the ancient logos of Coke and Pepsi.

We felt utterly alone, but in a split second, all that changed.

A dark car was approaching from the south, traveling way too fast. Tires screeched as it slid sideways into the gravel lot, coming to a stop three feet from the bumper of Liz's van.

"Mom!" I shouted, bolting upright, blood pounding in my ears. But before I could fully process the worst-case scenario that was playing through my mind, my best friend sat up straighter too and yelled, "Mom?" A second later, Bex was throwing open the van door and running to her mother, who was climbing out of the other car.

"Hello, darling," Mrs. Baxter said, throwing her arms around her daughter. But I noticed her gaze never left my mother's eyes.

"Anything, Grace?" Mom asked, climbing out of the van.

Bex's mother shook her head. "Nothing. You're clear."

At that moment a white pickup appeared on the deserted road, this time traveling from the north. It pulled into the abandoned station, and somehow I wasn't surprised at all to see Bex's father behind the wheel.

He hopped out of the truck. "All clear on my end, Rachel. You're free."

"Thanks, Abe." She sounded relieved, and to tell you the truth, I didn't like it. Because for there to be relief, there had to have been fear. And fear... well... I didn't want to think about that.

Liz poked me. "These are Bex's parents!"

I looked at my mother, who shrugged. "You didn't expect me not to recruit at least a little grown-up backup, did you?"

Macey stood on my other side and exclaimed, "We're going on a mission with Bex's parents!" as if wondering whether or not we were ready for Baxters to the power of three.

But my mother was shaking her head. "Actually, girls, for

unsanctioned ops, it's best to minimize the exposure of official agents."

It's a rule as old as espionage itself: Don't do yourself what you can get someone else to do for you. There are a million harmless reasons why a bunch of Gallagher Girls might break into Blackthorne (jokes, dares, pranks, etc.). For a bunch of grown-ups, not so much.

Bex knew all this—I know she did—and yet she was looking from my mother to hers, then back again. "So why are you . . ." she started, then trailed off.

"They're not here to *help* us." My voice was flat against the wind. "They're here to *guard* me." A look passed across my roommates' faces as if no time at all had passed since November—as if we were all still standing on a dark street in D.C.

"Do you have the journal?" Grace asked.

"No." Mom shook her head, then pointed to my roommates and me. "*They* beat me to it."

And that was when things got really weird.

I mean, *my mom* had broken into Sublevel Two!

My mom had been after my dad's journal.

My mom had been the person hot on our heels, creeping through the darkness in the depths of our school, which meant, I guess, that Agent Townsend hadn't been.

I was still shaking my head, trying to wrap my mind around that—around everything—when another car appeared on the highway, and Macey cried, "Abby?"

It sounded almost like a question, and with one glance at

my aunt I saw why. Her glossy hair had lost its shine. And when she walked toward us, the bounce that I had come to know in her step was gone.

"Hey, Squirt," she said, but it sounded forced. "Playing hooky, I see."

I shrugged. "Maybe this is a CoveOps field exercise?"

She raised an eyebrow. "I know Agent Townsend, Cams."

"Oh," Bex said.

"Which is why I am more than willing to take part in this little extracurricular assignment." She looked at her sister. "Well . . . one of the reasons."

My mom turned to Mr. Baxter. "What are our friends at Six saying, Abe?"

"Same story, different accent. No one has a bloody clue where they've taken him. No one seems to bloody care."

"I care."

Zach stood on the side of the dusty road, hands in pockets. When Mrs. Baxter saw him, she smiled a little too wide.

"Hello, Zachary," she said. "It's very nice to meet you. Rachel has told us . . . It's very nice to meet you."

Zach mumbled something that sounded like "You too." (I guess Blackthorne doesn't have a Madame Dabney.)

And then the time for pleasantries must have been over because Mrs. Baxter turned to my mom. "Ready?"

It seemed like the perfect question at the time. After all, I was getting ready to break into Blackthorne. I was out of the mansion. I was getting ready to go on a mission. A *real* mission. With Zach.

And my mom.

Words could not describe the nerves. Or the weirdness.

It occurred to me that I should have been taking notes, savoring every moment. But there was no time.

Mrs. Baxter started for the truck, climbing in beside her husband as she tossed my mother the keys to the sedan with the dark windows. Abby was already crawling into the SUV as Liz and Macey started for Liz's van, but my mother waved them away.

"It stays here," she said with a shake of her head. "We can't take the risk that someone might trace it back to you and the school."

When my mother turned to me and asked, "Do you have everything?" she sounded like she was dropping me off at school or a friend's house. She sounded almost like a normal mom.

When I said, "Yeah, we're ready," I sounded almost like a normal girl.

But as I watched my bodyguards pull onto the highway to monitor the perimeter of the school, normal felt completely overrated.

A moment later, my mother left us in a cloud of dust in the middle of nowhere, beside a gas station that had no gas, a van we couldn't drive, and a boy that some of the best spies in the world were hesitant to trust.

"And what are *we* supposed to do?" Macey asked.

Zach smiled. "We walk."

Chapter thirty-seven

It is a little-known fact about covert operations that you will spend a lot of time with people you can't really trust. They may be traitors and liars. We call them assets or informants. But mostly, in those days, I called him Zach.

The Operatives made contact with an asset who had firsthand knowledge of the Blackthorne Institute for Boys.

The Asset was also privy to Joe Solomon's private plans, the Circle's secrets, and some of the most awesome-smelling soap in the world.

The Operatives, therefore, tried not to trust (or smell) The Asset.

Walking across the weed-covered lot of the gas station, I could feel the darkness falling. The air was damp and chilly. I could hear Liz stumbling on the path behind me and knew without looking that Bex was bringing up the rear. I kept my eyes trained on the back of Zach's head as we walked deeper into the thick woods and closer to Blackthorne.

Twenty minutes later, I found myself asking, "How long until we get to the school?"

"Not long," Zach said, without breaking stride.

"How many guards will there be on patrol at our point of entry?"

He shrugged. "Don't know."

"What's the interval of the security camera sweep?"

"Hard to say."

I reached out for his arm in the dark. "What *do* you know, Zach?"

"You're on my home turf now, Gallagher Girl." His breath was warm on my skin. "Do you have a problem with that?"

"Guys..." I heard Liz's timid voice behind me.

"Maybe I do," I snapped back at Zach.

"Cam," Bex said, her voice mimicking the concern of Liz's, but I barely heard.

"Maybe I—" I started again, but before I could say another word, Bex grabbed my arm.

"Cam, listen!"

The forest was dark and still. Only the faintest hint of stars and moonlight shone through the dense canopy of trees.

I felt someone poke me, and I turned to looked at Bex, who raised one finger, as if to say, *listen closer*. And then I heard it: a distant rumble, low and steady, drifting through the trees.

Zach started walking, and the four of us followed until the

leaves overhead began to thin, and we were back under the open sky. Soon, we were staring over the side of a massive cliff, listening to a deafening roar.

"*What is that?*" Macey yelled, peering over the edge.

Zach didn't even glance at the river that raged beneath us, slicing through the wilderness two hundred feet below.

"That's our ride."

Anyone who's ever driven by the Gallagher Academy can see it standing safely behind its tall stone walls and strong fences. With one glance at the mountains that rose above us and the roaring river that raged below, I realized that the Blackthorne Institute had its own kind of walls. By the time we'd rappelled down the side of the cliff, persuaded Liz into a flimsy black rubber boat, and pushed into the current, I'd realized that the Gallagher Academy might have the best security money can buy, but what Blackthorne had was priceless. (Note to self: if you somehow get a *real* Covert Operations teacher before the end of the semester, this field op should be worth extra credit. *Lots* of extra credit.)

"Are you *sure* there's no other way in?" Liz asked. Her eyes were closed, and she was holding her second-favorite laptop, wrapped in a watertight case, as if her life depended on it.

Zach laughed. "Only the ones that sane people might use."

The whitecaps were coming faster. My fingers froze around my paddle, and as we crested a massive wave, Liz would have flown free had Bex and I not been there to grab her.

"And what's wrong with being sane?" Macey yelled through chattering teeth over the roar of the water.

Zach smiled and yelled, *"Insane means fewer cameras!"*

I didn't think it was possible, but in the next second I could have sworn the water started rushing faster. The roar became louder. Through the light of the moon, I could see the water stretching out before us, and then ... nothing. It was as if the river before us had fallen off the face of the earth.

"Zach ..." I didn't try to hide the panic in my voice. "Zach, why did the river disappear?" I asked, already dreading the answer. "Zach!"

And with that, the ground, the water, *everything* fell out from beneath us and we rushed over the falls. It was like a roller coaster—but faster. And wetter. And far less comfortable as we tumbled through the night sky, waiting for the splash.

How to Break Into Blackthorne
(A list by Operatives Morgan, Baxter, Sutton, and McHenry)

Step 1. Become slightly crazy.

Step 2. So crazy you actually volunteer to go over a fifty-foot waterfall.

Step 3. Swallow a lot of very cold river water.

Step 4. Cough and gag.

Step 5. Repeat Step 4 until it feels like maybe your lungs aren't inside your body anymore.

Step 6. Remember that a really cute boy is beside you, so try to cough in a far more attractive manner.

Step 7. Be grateful you're still alive.

———————

The first thought that came to me after the falling and the flailing and the gagging and the swimming and the "is everyone all right-ing" was that I was lying on my stomach on the river's rocky bank. There was a wide open field in front of me, while behind us, sheer, steep cliffs rose straight up into the sky and the river still roared deafeningly loud in our ears.

"No fences?" I asked.

Zach studied me. "No need." He pointed to the river and the cliffs. "Besides, this isn't the kind of place people are anxious to visit," he said flatly. I started to speak, but he cut me off. "You'll see."

Grandpa Morgan always says that to know a piece of grass, you've got to see the ground that grew it. Maybe that's why I remember every detail of that night, every inch of ground we covered, as I followed Zach to the place that had made him, seeing them both with fresh eyes.

In the moonlight, I could plainly see a long-distance rifle range thirty yards away. "Are those . . . ?"

"Yeah," Zach said, as if he didn't want to hear the rest of the question.

"How far away are the targets?" Bex asked.

Zach turned to us and whispered, "Far."

We passed a massive trench that had been hand-dug into the ground. Heavy ropes hung from the highest branches of tall trees. And beyond it all, there were muddy paths and rocky hills. I knew that despite the natural wonder of it, nothing about Blackthorne was beautiful; I knew that even in the sunshine, something about that place would always be a little dark.

Finally, we reached a fence that was at least fifteen feet tall. Moonlight glistened off the strands of barbed wire that circled at the top.

"Subtle," Bex said, staring up at it.

"This is the perimeter of the central grounds," Zach said. "As far as the general public knows, Blackthorne ends here. Follow the fence, and two hundred yards down you'll find a data access point that all of the electronic security runs through." He looked at Liz. "You know what you have to do?"

Liz beamed. "Yes."

"You're up to it? Because you're only going to have sixty seconds to run the hack. Sixty seconds or we don't make it in. Or back."

Liz looked insulted. "I know."

"She's got it," Macey told him.

Zach took a deep breath. "Yeah. I know. I'm just . . . It looks different from this side, you know?"

Not for the first time, I wondered whether or not Zach had dropped out of school at Blackthorne, where he was living, how he was surviving, but this didn't seem like the time to ask questions. He probably wouldn't have answered anyway.

"Security between here and there?" Bex asked.

"Walk softly and you'll be fine."

Still, my three best friends in the world looked concerned.

"Bex and Liz can handle the perimeter," Macey said, turning to me. "Maybe I should come with you."

"The more people who go, the more likely we get seen," I countered.

"Yeah," Zach said. "Which is exactly why you should stay here."

"You said yourself you don't know exactly what's in there, Zach. Going in without backup is foolish."

"Then let me be foolish."

"No."

"Why?"

"Because I have to *do something*, okay? I can't sit tight and . . . be patient. . . . I need to *do* something."

No one said anything for a moment. We were all too wet, too sore, and we'd come entirely too far to turn back.

Then Macey stared right into Zach's eyes. "We're leaving her with you," she warned.

"I'll be fine, Macey," I said, but it was as if she hadn't heard a word.

"We're leaving her with *you*," she said again. "And if you make us regret that . . ."

"*I won't*," Zach said, and somehow I believed him.

The Operative was led through a series of gates, doors, and really muddy ditches. The Operative did

218

not, however, complain about ruining her favorite jeans. (Even though she really, really wanted to.)

On the other side of the chain-link fence, I guess I thought the world would change. And it did. Just not in the ways I was expecting.

I have seen the Gallagher Academy on the coldest of nights and the hottest days. I have crawled through its deepest passageways and stared out of the highest windows. I have walked across it in deep snow and heavy rain.

I *know* what a spy school looks like!

Or, at least, I thought I did. Until then.

Zach and I lay on our stomachs at the top of a low ridge, staring down at the Blackthorne Institute for Boys through the glare of a searchlight that swept across the grounds from the school's tallest tower. Most of the buildings were low and square with metal roofs and heavy grates on every window.

Despite the hour, a group of twenty boys was running across the open field that lay between the tree-covered hill and the big square buildings. They wore yellow jumpsuits and ran in perfect unison, marching, really, their chanting cries echoing through the valley in the dark.

"Night drills," Zach whispered, but drills for what, I didn't dare to ask.

A pair of headlights appeared at the gates, shining past the guard station and onto the gravel lane.

"Mom," I whispered.

"Right on time," Zach said.

When my mother began the drive toward the main buildings, I lifted my binoculars and carefully studied the sign that hung on the gate that swung open. BLACKTHORNE INSTITUTE FOR BOYS, PRIVATE DETENTION FACILITY. DANGER. NO TRESPASSING BEYOND THIS POINT.

The last year flooded back in bits and pieces—the perfectly made beds in the boys' temporary quarters in the East Wing; the way the boys had twitched and squirmed as if they'd never worn a suit jacket or a tie in their lives; and, most of all, the look in Zach's eyes as he'd warned me that I wouldn't like life at his school—wouldn't like it at all.

"You've got your cover, Gallagher Girl," Zach said quietly. "We've got ours."

Upon gaining access to the Blackthorne Institute for Boys, The Operatives were able to ascertain the following:

- The Blackthorne Institute's firewalls, according to Operative Sutton, were good. But not quite good enough.
- As a part of their cover, the residents of the Blackthorne Institute were forced to wear jumpsuits in a shade of yellow that, according to Operative McHenry, doesn't look good on ANYONE.
- The guards at the Blackthorne Institute utilized a fairly aggressive form of perimeter patrol that

was very effective except when an intruder knows the Bazinsky Method (which Operative Baxter did).

Zach had been right, of course. His school wasn't like my school. Blackthorne tried to look like a place for thugs, and the Gallagher Academy appeared to be a palace for princesses. My school was a half mile from Highway 10. Zach's school was hidden in the mountains, shielded from the outside world.

They had barbed wire, and we had stone walls.

Their school looked like a prison made to keep people in, and my school appeared to be a mansion built to keep people out.

But as I lay with Zach in the dark at the top of the ridge, I heard him breathing. His arm was warm against mine, and I feared I might sweat or fidget, that he might feel the blood that was pumping too fast through my body and guess the thoughts that were raging inside of me—all the things I didn't trust him to see or know.

I tried to pull away, but he put his hands on my shoulders and held me there. I knew that the Blackthorne Institute lay just beyond that ridge with its guards and teachers and little Joe-Solomons-in-training, and yet it felt like Zach and I were the only people on earth as he pressed his body against mine.

His hands moved to cup my face, and in the faint traces of light, I saw his eyes perhaps more clearly than I ever had.

Zach saw me.

Zach knew me.

I was anything but invisible as we lay in the shadows, his face inches away from mine.

"Stay here," he whispered. I felt the words brush across my skin. "Please, Gallagher Girl, just stay here."

I wanted to pull away, to remind him that I was a big girl, a highly trained operative, a spy—that I'd been training for this mission my entire life, and I wasn't going to be left on the sidelines. But in the dim space with Zach pressed tightly against me, only one thought came to mind. I kissed him—longer and deeper than I ever had before. The school was not watching us this time. There was nothing playful in the tone. We were just two people kissing as if for the first time, as if it might be the last.

And then I broke away. "So," I asked, as if I got kissed like that all the time (which, believe me, I don't), "where is it you're taking me again?"

"The tombs."

Chapter thirty-eight

In the next twenty minutes, I broke maybe a dozen rules of covert operations.

After all, I didn't know where we were going. I had no idea what we were going to find when we got there. I hadn't planned alternate entry strategies, exit strategies, or strategies for keeping my ponytail from blowing in my face. All I knew for certain was that Zach's hand was gripping mine (despite verifiable research that people are way stealthier when holding on to nothing), and that Bex's voice was the only familiar thing I could hear.

"Chameleon, what did he say again?" she asked through the comms unit in my ear as Zach and I covered the open ground beyond the ridge at a full run. "Because we're searching the database for 'tombs,' but—"

"It's not *in* the database," Zach cut in.

"Is it some kind of cemetery? We can't find an entrance on the—"

"There are no recorded entrances."

"Or references to it anywhere," Bex finished.

Zach looked at me. "It's not the kind of place that gets referenced."

"Cameras passing in three, two, drop!" Liz commanded from her watch post, and Zach and I fell to the ground like stones.

"Roll," Liz said, and I propelled myself down a steep incline and landed in a muddy ditch.

I heard voices coming from above us, footsteps as the Blackthorne Boys ran past in perfect unison, while Zach and I continued crawling through the mud.

"Wait, it's not an actual tomb, is it?" Macey asked. It seemed like an excellent question, but Zach was silent, still crawling away from the buildings and the guards, and toward the mountain that formed the backdrop of the school.

"What are the tombs, Zach?" I asked again when we reached the base of the first hill and climbed out of the ditch and into the shelter of the trees. The ground was rough and steep. We walked along a path that was overgrown with weeds and brush—as if the wilderness were trying to reclaim it.

"Guys, you're clear now," Liz said from two miles away, but I'd already sensed it.

The marching boys were gone. No cameras could possibly reach us through the dense canopy of trees.

Only a single ray of moonlight sliced through the limbs. I remember that now—how I could so plainly see the features of Zach's face, the look in his eyes as he started pushing aside the moss-covered rocks that sat on the steep mountainside.

"What are you looking for?"

"There should be an entrance around here somewhere." He kicked at the dead leaves and fallen brush that covered the forest floor. "It'll be hidden—made to blend in. But there should be a switch, or maybe..."

"A lever?" I asked, walking three feet to a tree that grew from the steep mountainside at an angle unlike any of the others. I reached for the only limb in the entire forest that didn't have a single new leaf. "You mean like this one?"

"Caves?" I heard my own voice echo, even though the word had been barely louder than a whisper. "The tombs are caves?"

"Watch your step," was Zach's answer.

I could still hear my roommates chattering in my ear, but the sound dissolved deeper into static with every step behind the hidden door.

The stone walls around us were close and damp, lit by bare, dim bulbs that hung at regular intervals. I had a feeling that we weren't going underground. It was more like we were going straight through the mountains that were the Blackthorne Institute's first and perhaps best line of defense.

"The Native Americans indigenous to this area used to bury their dead in caves like this," Zach offered out of the blue. "That's why they call them the tombs. The army used this whole area for weapons testing and training in World War Two. After the war, they found another use for it."

It was strange hearing Zach offer up anything about his past. I wanted to ask for more, but stayed quiet, remembering summers on the ranch and how the baby calves would creep close sometimes, curious and timid, uncertain whom to trust. I knew if I moved too fast I might scare him away, so I just waited.

"We don't really..." He looked at me. "We don't really use them anymore."

"How far do they go?" I asked, mesmerized.

"Far."

"How many branches and offshoots are there?"

"A lot."

"Are you going to tell me why you were so desperate to keep me out of here?" I asked.

He stopped suddenly, and I ran into his chest. It was almost as hard as the stone walls around us.

"You'll see for yourself soon enough."

We walked for what felt like hours, disabling booby traps and dodging surveillance cameras.

"Maybe we should split up," I suggested.

"You stay with me," Zach said, like it wasn't really up for debate.

The passageway was taller than the ones at the Gallagher Academy. The concrete walls felt more modern. It was a next-generation tunnel, to be sure; but it wasn't new or nice. Nothing about it was anything but functional, and the dank smell and thick cobwebs told me that it hadn't really functioned in a very long time.

"Watch your step," Zach warned when we reached a sloping

portion of the tunnel where water congealed in thick black pools.

"Oh, I bet you say that to all the girls you bring down here."

Zach stopped. When he turned, he didn't even look like the boy I knew. "*No one* comes down here."

Five feet ahead, the stone passageway widened. The ceilings rose taller. I could hear the steady drip, drip, drip of water seeping through the cracks in the stone above us and falling into puddles on a concrete floor. But there were no soft edges there, no bright lights. Stepping inside, I realized that we have our fair share of secret underground chambers at the Gallagher Academy, but I had never been anyplace like this.

Chains dangled from the tall ceilings along one wall. A collection of dummies with crude red circles painted on their chests lined another. Stainless-steel tables stood in the middle of the room while cobweb-covered trays with syringes and pliers sat waiting, as if someone might walk in at any moment, brush aside the dust, and continue with some terrible experiment.

"We don't use it anymore," Zach said, his voice soft despite the fact that there wasn't a soul who could have overheard us. Shame seeped into his words as he looked at the damp concrete floor. "We really *don't* use it anymore."

A half dozen other passageways opened into this room, and yet I felt the mountain pressing down on me as if there were no way out.

"Zach . . ." My voice caught in my throat. "What is this place?"

"You really don't know what kind of school this is, do you?"

"It's a *spy* school," I snapped, blood pounding in my veins.

He shook his head slowly. Even in the dim light I saw his eyes go wide. "Not spies. Not always."

"Then what?"

"Come on, Gallagher Girl—a school in the middle of nowhere for troubled boys with no other place to go? You *know* what this place is."

I looked at the room around us, thought about the rifle ranges and marching boys, about the hours my roommates and I had spent last spring searching for any clue about Blackthorne and finding nothing but secrets and lies.

"No," I said. "Mr. Solomon went here. He—"

"Was starting to change things," Zach finished. He stepped closer. "You know what we are, Gallagher Girl."

"No." I shook my head. "You can't be . . ."

There are a lot of terms for what Zach was trying to say. *Killers. Wet work artists.* But all I could do was look at the boy who stood beside me—the boy I barely knew—and whisper, "*Assassins.*"

"I told you this place was made to prepare for war—World War Two, the Cold War, and all the wars that could have happened but didn't. Or haven't yet." He stared at me, almost pleading as he whispered, "We *don't* use it anymore."

"Is this why they don't trust you? The Baxters . . . Aunt Abby—"

"Are smart people with good instincts." He looked away, then back again.

"But that doesn't make any sense, Zach. You didn't build this place. What could you have possibly done that is so terrible?"

"No!" Standing there, hundreds of feet into the mountain, there was no way to know how far the shout reverberated through the maze of stone.

"Really. You can tell me."

"No. I really can't."

Upon learning the original purpose of the Blackthorne Institute for Boys, The Operative thought she might more easily understand The Asset.

(But it turns out, potential future assassin-slash-spy boys are the most confusing boys of all.)

It took another hour to reach it. Twice we found the tunnels blocked by a cave-in, a hundred tons of stone standing in our way. Once, Zach admitted we were on the wrong path, and we had to backtrack a hundred yards. We passed three more rooms like the first we'd seen—a dozen locked doorways and concrete bunkers so dark I couldn't see a thing.

"I've never been this deep," he admitted. Somehow, I knew exactly how he felt.

"Not to sound ungrateful or anything, but do you know where we're going?"

He smiled for what felt like the first time in hours. "Not exactly." He reached for my hand, bent to ease beneath a low-hanging arch. "Joe told me where he left it, just in case . . . in case of this."

"And where's that?" I asked, but Zach stopped.

He pointed. "In there."

The room was large—two stories tall with at least a half dozen tunnels spiraling off of it. Somehow, just standing there, I knew we'd finally reached the center of the mountain.

As Zach and I stepped onto a small metal landing on the second story, I looked down on the room below us. It was crude and basic. Metal stairs ran down to the lower floor. Shelves and filing cabinets lined the walls. And on every inch of surface there were files and boxes and relics of the past.

"It's . . ." Zach started slowly. "It's sort of like Blackthorne's version of Sublevel Two."

I followed him down the stairs and watched him go to the far side of the room and squat down beside a rusty shelf. I held my breath as he reached, stretching as far as he could, then pulled out a spiral notebook wrapped tightly in plastic.

"That's *it?*" I asked. It looked so plain—like a million other notebooks carried by a million other kids. Finally, I truly understood the fact I'd known for months: *Joe Solomon had been sixteen.*

Zach tucked the journal into his belt and under his jacket, then took my hand. Wordlessly, we climbed the metal stairs and started back down the tunnel from which we'd come.

It seemed so easy. Our mission was over. We'd won.

But that was when we heard the voices.

Chapter THiRtY-nine

My first thought was that the Blackthorne security team had found us—that we'd missed a motion sensor or tripped a silent alarm—and I started preparing my excuses. . . . Zach was my boyfriend. I was there on a dare. Breaking into Blackthorne was the best extra credit project ever!

But then Zach and I dropped to our stomachs and crawled back to the metal landing that overlooked the massive storage space below, and . . .

And I saw the woman from the roof.

There was no mistaking her this time, because there, in the tombs, everything was louder, sharper, my senses were more alive than they had ever been before as I lay staring at the woman who had found me on a rooftop in Boston. And she was not alone.

Mr. Solomon's hands were bound. One of his eyes was bruised and swollen so badly it was completely shut, and as he limped forward I saw a massive gash in his left leg. Five men stood guard around him.

"Okay," the woman said, turning to Mr. Solomon. "Now where is it?"

"What?"

The woman struck Mr. Solomon's face so hard that blood sprayed across the room.

"I'm only going to ask you one more time." The woman moved closer. In the hollow stone room, her whisper seemed to echo. "Where is the log book that belonged to Matthew Morgan?"

My *dad's* journal. They were looking for Dad's journal.

But Dad's journal wasn't here, and Mr. Solomon knew that —Mr. Solomon knew everything about this place and yet he'd brought them into the depths of the mountain.

Into Blackthorne's version of Sublevel Two.

Beside me, I could feel the tension in Zach's arms. I could sense the gears working in his mind as we both asked a single question: What would Joe Solomon do?

"No," Zach gasped. I followed his gaze.

Cables lined the ceiling and walls, disappearing behind the shelves and filing cabinets, connecting everything in the room to a box labeled WARNING: EXPLOSIVES, and I couldn't help thinking, *Just like Sublevel Two. . . .*

I didn't know Joe Solomon—after all I'd learned about him, I wondered if I ever really would. But I knew that he would never willingly give in to the Circle again. I knew he would trade his life to bring the Circle to its end.

I looked at the explosives that filled the room—the burn bag they were locked inside of—and knew that Mr. Solomon hadn't come here to save his life but to end it, and hopefully, take as many of them out as possible.

Zach started to stand, but I grabbed him.

"Think, Zach." I held him there. "We only have one chance."

I watched as fury faded into fear, and Zach stared into my eyes. "Cammie, you have to take this." He pressed the plastic-covered notebook into my hands. "You have to run."

"No. I have to help him."

He squeezed my hands tighter. "You have to *live*. Now go, and don't look back for anything."

"But, Zach—"

"They won't hurt me."

I wanted to ask why, but I knew he wouldn't say. I wanted to ask how, but I knew it didn't matter. Despite my training and good sense, I wanted to argue, but I knew we were out of time. Because A) There's very little use in arguing with a spy who has made up his or her mind. And B) Three armed men stood blocking the tunnel behind us, and there was absolutely no way out.

When the woman saw us, she laughed. It was a haunting, echoing sound there in the middle of that mountain.

"Found them on a sweep," the guard said, dragging me down the stairs. I tried to pull free, but the man was holding me too tightly. The woman walked closer, staring at me. Appraising me. It was the dirtiest I'd ever felt in my life.

"Oh, this is a surprise." She smiled at my teacher. "Joe, you clever boy, why didn't you tell me you were bringing me a present?"

I looked at Mr. Solomon—tried to say that I was sorry. That I had followed the pigeons, but I'd failed. I expected to see disappointment in my teacher's remaining good eye, but instead what I saw was rage.

"They go or I give you nothing!"

"Now why would I do that?" the woman asked. "Break up this touching reunion?"

She reached out her hand, and I thought for a second that she was going to stroke my hair, but at the last minute she shifted, reached for Zach's cheek, and said, "Hello, sweetheart. Aren't you going to introduce your little girlfriend to your mother?"

Chapter forTy

The mind is a powerful thing. I've read the research. I've seen it in action. My whole life had taught me those simple facts, and yet, in that moment, there was one thing my mind couldn't start to comprehend: the woman from the roof in Boston was Zach's mother.

I wanted to be sick.

"She's your mother," I stated plainly. It wasn't a question—it was a data point, and Zach was slowly, somehow, making sense.

He reached for me. "Gallagher Girl—"

"Don't touch me." I pulled away, but not before his fingers grazed my skin, before I felt a spark, and I swore it would be the last thing I'd feel for him ever again.

In my ear, the comms unit was silent. We'd searched for too long, gone too far, and now there was entirely too much mountain between me and any kind of help.

"It is very nice to finally meet you, Cammie. I've heard

so much about you." When Zach's mother spoke, she sounded serene. "I hope you're not afraid. I'm sure Joe here would gladly confirm that we don't want to kill you."

My heart was racing, and yet somehow I knew that it was true—they really *didn't* want to hurt me. Which meant they wanted something far, far worse.

"Cammie, I—" Again, Zach reached for me. Again, I pulled away.

"Oh, sweetheart, I can see why you like her." His mother laughed. "But now, everyone spread out and look for Morgan's diary." She eyed her son and me. "And someone search the two of them."

A guard was still holding me. Another man was moving closer. Through the light of the dim bulb that hung in the middle of the tall ceiling, I saw Zach's eyes go wide, and I thought of all the times he'd looked at me before—on an elevator in D.C., in the town square in Roseville, and in a tiny compartment on a train barreling through the night.

But as the guard reached me, an entirely new face was staring at me, whispering, "Now!"

Believe it or not, there are some advantages to fighting two attackers instead of one. It was so much easier to throw my weight back against the man who held me and kick the guard who was walking forward with his hands outstretched.

From the corner of my eye, I saw Zach was spinning, kicking one of the ancient filing cabinets in the direction of his mother. It crashed against her, knocking her to the floor, paper falling all around her, while the guard at my back pushed me aside as if I were nothing, and ran to his boss's aid.

"What are you doing?" the woman yelled. "Get her!"

I heard the words. Felt my vision go blurry with rage. And in the next second, a dozen things seemed to happen at once.

Mr. Solomon lunged toward one of the men near the entrance of another tunnel. My teacher threw his bound hands over the man's head and strangled him, while I ran with all my might in their direction.

Someone moved to block my path, but I jumped onto the bookcase, used my momentum to flip midair and catch the man's chin with my foot, before dropping lightly to the ground. But someone else appeared in the corner of my eye, and I moved just as Zach's mother placed a kick inches from my ear.

I stepped back as she circled me. Like I was prey. Above us, that lone lightbulb swayed, casting a moving shadow over everything it touched as the woman who'd been haunting my dreams for months moved closer to me and smiled.

"You're far prettier up close, you know."

I parried away another of her blows, and when I countered, I landed a swift punch to her kidney and another to her face.

"Oh yes," she said, wiping at the blood that trickled from the side of her mouth. "I can certainly see the appeal."

"Forgive me if I can't say the same," I managed to quip.

Across the room, Zach had taken an old sword from the wall and was fighting two men at once. The steel blade made a sharp sound in the hollow space and the rhythmic clash of the blades was almost soothing—like a beat. A pulse.

"You know, Cammie, I do wish you and I could be friends. We have so much in common."

"Yeah, I—" But then I couldn't finish, because I realized that the swords were no longer clashing. I turned to see that the two men Zach had been fighting were now on the ground, bleeding, struggling to their feet, while Zach dashed to Mr. Solomon, who was fighting on the other side of the room.

Zach was so focused on Mr. Solomon, so anxious to come to our teacher's aid, that he didn't see when one of the men on the ground pulled out a gun and took aim at Zach's back.

"No!" someone screamed, and only when the man stopped did I realize that it hadn't been me. There was only one person in that cave with the power to save Zach—one person with the power to stop those dominoes from falling, and she was the person who turned from me and started toward her son.

I watched Zach's mother slam into the gunman—heard the weapon clatter across the floor. Even without turning, I knew that no one was behind me then—that there was absolutely nothing between me and one of the tunnels that spiraled off the main floor. And yet I couldn't move.

Everything seemed to freeze for that one second, as Zach picked up the gun and yelled, "Now! Run!"

But I couldn't leave him, couldn't run, couldn't do anything but shout "No!" as Zach took aim at the metal box marked WARNING: EXPLOSIVES, and mouthed the word, "Good-bye."

The shot echoed through the tombs. Sparks rained down, lighting up the cave like the Fourth of July. A red light sizzled past me while my arms started pumping at my sides, the journal rubbing against the small of my back. And even when the first crack of the explosion sounded through the tombs, I managed to stay ahead of it, one foot in front of the other through the eerie, smoky haze.

I kept running.

I didn't look back.

No good would come from watching as the ghosts of Blackthorne burned.

Chapter forty-One

Fire. I tried to forget about the fire, but the narrow tunnels felt like an oven. The water seeping through the walls turned to steam. I didn't let myself think about the caved-in passages that Zach and I had seen, and the chance that this unfamiliar tunnel was a dead end too. I just kept running until the smoke grew thinner and the air was fresher.

"Spread out!" The call echoed through the dark. "Find her!"

In my ear, the comms unit was beginning to crack and hum, and I spoke into the static, "I'm in the tombs. I'm running... I don't know." But I *did* know. Mr. Solomon was dead, but his voice was still alive in my mind. "South. I'm running south. The Circle is behind me."

I heard my mother's voice shouting orders, but not to me. I ran faster. Toward the light. Toward the woods. Toward fresh air and freedom and backup. It would be over soon. All I had to do was keep running.

The sound of the river was louder. I could hear the falls and breathe the moist, fresh air.

"I'm almost clear," I yelled into my comms. "I'm almost—"

But then I turned the corner, skidded to a stop, and realized I wasn't near the falls—I was *behind* them.

The tunnel ended in a rocky cliff. Gushing, falling water was the only thing standing between me and sky.

"I'm behind the waterfall," I shouted. "I'm—"

"Trapped?"

The woman didn't look like Zach—not then, not really. Without the mask she'd worn in Boston, I could see that her hair was a dark red and her skin was as pale as Madame Dabney's finest china. Her eyes, though. She had the same dark eyes as her son. As she looked at me, I couldn't shake the feeling that I'd never see his again.

"It's over," I told her. "I'm wearing a comms unit. Everyone knows—"

"It doesn't matter what your protection detail knows, Cammie dear. It's too late. No one can help you."

I heard more sounds coming from behind her. People were coming. Her people.

"You can't beat us," I said. "Kill me, take me, it doesn't matter. The Gallagher Academy will just make more girls like me. If one of us lives, we all live."

"Of course they will." She smiled. "They made *me*."

I didn't say anything—I swear I really didn't—but the look on my face must have spoken volumes, because in the next moment, the woman was laughing a terrible, joyless laugh.

"Oh, didn't Zach ever mention that his mother was a Gallagher Girl?" She cocked an eyebrow, then shrugged. "I guess not."

"No." I shook my head. "No. Gallagher Girls are—"

"We're whatever we want to be, Cammie." She stepped closer. I cringed at the word *we*. "*Anything* we want to be."

I thought about what Abby and the Baxters had said that night in the castle—that the Circle had a knack for recruiting agents very young. . . . Joe Solomon had grown up and seen the light and spent his life trying to right his wrongs. But most people—I looked at Zach's mother, at the dark depths of her eyes—most never left the tombs.

"So, see? We're sisters, Cammie. You really don't have to be afraid. What we need lives *inside* of you." She tapped her temple. "We only want to borrow it."

Mr. Solomon was dead.

Zach was dead.

"I won't go with you," I said, easing closer to the edge, remembering her promise and the fact that had haunted me for months: They wanted me alive.

"Come on, Cammie, step away from that nasty cliff. Don't be foolish."

"I'm not foolish," I said, more certain of anything than I'd ever been in my life.

The sound of the water was deafening. The back of my

shirt was wet with mist. I wanted to wipe the water from my eyes, but I needed my hands in front of me. I needed to be ready.

"You don't want to do this, Cammie. We really *aren't* going to hurt you."

"I know," I said, and I did. Sort of.

"We just want to take you someplace—ask you some questions. Help you...*remember*...some things."

"I'm sure you do." I moved, and the rocks at my feet crumbled.

Mr. Solomon was dead.

Zach was dead.

Her own son was dead, and still she was chasing me and whatever secret I carried.

I had been studying Protection and Enforcement for five and a half years, but until that moment I'd never seriously thought what it would feel like to kill someone—until then I'd never wanted to.

"What?" she asked. "What are you thinking?"

"I'm trying to decide whether or not I should kill you."

She laughed. "You can't kill me."

But I could. At that moment I was so full of fear and rage and grief that I could have done it. Easily.

She laughed harder and stepped slowly closer, as if that wall of water and air were the worst possible fate.

And then Zach's mother leaned close, as if confiding, and said, "If you kill *me*, then who will take you to your father?"

She lunged for me, but I was the one who no longer had anything to lose.

And before her words had found a place in my mind—before the Circle operatives who were rushing down the tunnel could reach us—I thought about the ravens, and I spread my wings to fly.

Chapter forty-two

The jump didn't kill me, in case you don't already know.

I remember breaking through the falls.

I remember fresh air and the cold wind and thinking I could fly.

And then there was the crash and the freezing currents that fell over and over and over me like a blanket I was trapped inside as I fought to break free.

And then there was nothing. No more blackness. No fire. No heat and no cold.

And for the first time in months I slept and did not dream.

"Cammie!"

I heard my name echo through the night, riding on the wind. My body ached. My clothes clung to me, heavy and wet. I could hear the river and the yells and something else, a voice inside of me telling me it wasn't safe. The Circle was still out there.

I had to move. I had to hide. I thought about the last thing Zach had ever asked of me: I had to keep running and I could never, ever look back.

Not when I heard the helicopter.

Not when I saw the spotlight sweeping across the open ground along the river and then burning me, holding me steady in its glare.

Not when I heard the deep voice yell, "I have her! She's here!"

Not when the strong arms wrapped around me, and someone said, "Hold still."

Not even when the black chopper landed on the ground in front of me, and my mother flew from its open door.

I had to keep running even then, but my feet no longer met the ground. I tried to fight, but the arms that held me were too strong.

"Rachel," Agent Townsend said, still gripping me.

"Cammie, sweetheart, stop fighting," my mother said as my teacher carried me beneath the whirling blades.

Chapter FORTY-THREE

It was loud inside the helicopter. I tried to move, but the entire right side of my body was on fire.

Fire.

"Mr. Solomon," I started, but the words were strangled in a cough, as if my lungs had carried the explosion with them. "Zach..."

"Sweetheart, your shoulder is dislocated. There's going to be a great deal of pain when the shock wears off."

What shock? I wanted to say, but I reached for my mother's hand instead.

"Dad," I whispered. "She was going to take me to Dad."

"She's hallucinating, Rachel." Agent Townsend was talking above me. He and my mother were talking about me.

"He's alive!" I bolted upright and a pain like I'd never known shot through me. "They're dead," I mumbled, but everything was swirling, fading into black.

* * *

Upon admission to the Gallagher Academy infirmary, Operative Morgan was poked, prodded, shot, scanned, X-rayed, and bandaged.

She was not, however, questioned, interrogated, debriefed, or told what the heck was going on.

"Mom?" My voice was so scratchy, I barely recognized it as my own. "Is my mother here?"

"No." Someone behind me spoke. I heard the door close, watched Agent Townsend walk to the foot of my metal bed. "She isn't."

I might have been drugged and bruised and bandaged, but the irony wasn't lost on me. I knew we hadn't come very far since London.

"I want to talk to my mother."

"She can't be here at the moment, Ms. Morgan. I'm afraid you'll have to start with me."

"I can wait."

He smiled. "But I can't. You see, I have a plane to catch."

Okay, so maybe it was the drugs they had me on, but that almost sounded like good news.

I tried to sit upright, but my body didn't want to obey. My shoulder ached, and my right side was one continuous, massive bruise.

"Nothing's broken," he said, as if it were a miracle, and I guess it really was. "But you're going to be sore for a while. The fall dislocated your shoulder and you inhaled a lot of smoke, but you're going to be okay, young lady."

He sat down in the metal chair at the foot of my bed. "Now, tell me what happened in the tombs."

I told him everything—I really did. From finding out the truth about Blackthorne to the sight of the Circle dragging Mr. Solomon back to the place that, in a way, had started it all.

I told it in detail and in order.

Joe Solomon would have been extremely proud.

As I talked, Agent Townsend listened, but he didn't take a single note—he didn't say a single word.

"And then I jumped," I told him finally. I looked down at my bruised body. "I guess . . . I guess you know the rest."

He nodded slowly. "Yes. I suppose I might even know a bit more than you." He placed his elbows on his knees and leaned closer.

"They've pulled three bodies from the wreckage so far, and they're still digging. Your roommates are completely unharmed, although probably more than a little irate that they're being kept from you," he added, as if the drama of teenage girls was seriously starting to weigh on him.

Then he leaned closer, his voice low as he added, "And something else."

He walked to the door and came back with a wheelchair. A minute later Agent Townsend was pushing me into a dim room that was larger than my own. Machines beeped. Nurses and doctors moved with noiseless steps. And in the center of it all, a man lay on a bed, broken and burned, one eye swollen completely shut.

"A young man brought him here late last night. He has no ID. No name." As Townsend pushed me closer, I felt myself stop breathing. The man on the bed was bandaged almost from head to toe, and yet when the wheelchair stopped, I saw a face I'd first seen at the back of the Grand Hall a year and a half before.

"So perhaps we'll just call him . . . Mr. S."

I wanted to take his hand, but I didn't want to touch him and risk finding out it was a dream.

"Now, if you'll excuse me, Ms. Morgan," Townsend said. "I'm afraid I really must be leaving. MI6 has a lot of questions, as you might imagine, and I—"

"But—"

"My job here was to find Joe Solomon, young lady." He looked at me for a long time. "And Joe Solomon is dead. Witnesses saw him die in an explosion just last night." Tears swelled in my eyes, but I didn't try to stop him. I didn't say thank you or I'm sorry or any of a dozen other things that Agent Townsend probably had no desire to hear.

Instead, I watched him look at the man in the bed—the man who'd come closer to destroying the Circle than anyone alive. I saw him nod at Mr. Solomon and heard him whisper, "There's no need for anyone to chase him anymore."

Townsend was halfway to the door when he stopped.

"Oh yes," he said, turning. "You were clutching this last night." He pulled the small spiral-bound notebook from his pocket and handed it to me. I almost didn't recognize it without its plastic wrapping. "Interesting choice of books you have there, Ms. Morgan." He turned slowly around. "Most interesting indeed."

"How long have you been chasing the Circle, Agent Townsend?" I called suddenly, stopping him at the door.

"A long time," he said.

"Do you think my father is with them? Do you think he's alive?"

His voice was flat as he said, "No."

Then he turned and walked away.

Chapter forty-four

"Hey, kiddo," my mother said from behind me. But instead of turning, I stayed seated, staring at Mr. Solomon, wondering, not for the first time, if I was looking at a ghost.

"Is he . . . Is he going to make it?" I asked.

"It's too soon to say, sweetheart," Mom admitted. She moved closer. "How are you?"

But I didn't answer. Instead, I turned and asked, "Where's Zach? He's the one who brought Mr. Solomon back, isn't he? Is he here? Is he—"

"He's fine, kiddo. A little burned. A little bruised. But he'll be fine. And yes, he's here." She inched closer. "In fact, I've been on the phone with the trustees all morning, getting their permission for him to finish the semester with us." She took a deep breath. "There's no place safe for him to go."

As she talked, her hands went almost involuntarily to Mr. Solomon—straightening his blanket, smoothing his bandages—and I knew that, unlike me, she couldn't stop touching him. She would heal him with her bare hands if she could.

"Dad's alive."

And just like that, my mother pulled her hand away.

"He's alive, Mom," I said, cursing the wheelchair, needing to face my mother and the world head-on and not like an invalid, like a child. "He's alive. She...Zach's mother said so."

Mom sank to her knees and looked into my eyes. "Listen to me, Cammie. *Listen*. They will say anything—they will do anything to get what they want. And what they want right now is you."

"Why?" I asked, the question burning inside of me. "They came to Blackthorne because Mr. Solomon told them Dad's journal was there. They'd go anywhere to find me. *What do they want?*"

Mom smoothed my hair. "We don't know, kiddo. I think your father was probably getting close to something. I think that's why they killed him."

"She said he's alive!"

"Don't let yourself be fooled, Cammie!" my mother snapped, then dropped her voice to a whisper. "Don't let yourself...hope."

I know too well how dangerous hope can be, how it grows and sometimes dies, taking its host with it. It's more powerful than anything Dr. Fibs keeps in his labs, more precious than all the secrets inside Sublevel Two.

"Maybe she wasn't lying," I said. "Right? Tell me she might not be lying."

"We don't know." She said each word slowly, carefully, as if they were as much for her as for me. "But I've spent years looking for your father and I think—in my professional opinion—he probably isn't . . . alive."

Operatives who always lie make the worst spies. Their intel is discounted, their missions are abandoned. There always has to be some truth among the scraps. Covert Operatives call it chicken feed. But in that room on that day, my mother simply called it hope.

As my mother pushed my wheelchair to the door, I handed her the old spiral-bound notebook. "Mr. Solomon wanted Zach to have this. Can you see that he gets it?"

"Give it to him yourself, kiddo. He's waiting right outside."

His face was still covered with soot and ash. His clothes had been singed. There were bandages on his right arm, and yet everything about Zach was perfect. He had come through it all unscathed. Alive.

My mom pushed me toward him, but he didn't take my hand. We didn't hug or kiss. The fire somehow was still between us, and neither of us moved toward the other, afraid we might get burned.

"Here. You should have this." I held out the journal. "When he wakes up . . ."

He reached for the journal. His fingers brushed mine.

There were a million things to say, or maybe more, but the feeling of his skin was enough in that brief moment. We were warm. We were alive.

"Cam!" My roommates' voices echoed down the hallway, followed by the sounds of hurried footsteps against the hardwood floors.

"Cammie, we were so worried!" Liz cried. Bex and Macey threw their arms around me with slightly more force than someone should use on a person who has a full-body bruise and a dislocated shoulder.

"I'm okay, guys," I pleaded. "I'm fine. Zach and I are—"

But then I trailed off. I turned to look behind me and saw nothing but an empty hall.

Chapter forty-five

PROS AND CONS OF THE LAST FEW
WEEKS OF OUR JUNIOR YEAR

PRO: Bex's mom volunteered to take a temporary leave from MI6 to teach CoveOps for the rest of the semester.

CON: Mr. Solomon was still sleeping.

PRO: Turns out, when a current Gallagher Girl gets seriously injured by an ex (and evil) Gallagher Girl, other Gallagher Girls from all over the world send awesome get-well presents —like chocolate. From Switzerland.

CON: Your roommates' new "Cammie doesn't go anywhere without *two* of us" rule means the chocolates don't last very long. At all.

PRO: Being on the P&E "Cautious Practice" roster gives a girl lots of time to work on her crossbow skills.

CON: Crossbow practice almost always includes Liz (who

only *grazed* Madame Dabney that one time, no matter what you might have heard).

PRO: An incredibly smart, incredibly hot, incredibly mysterious boy had come to the Gallagher Academy.

CON: Not one of us could let ourselves forget why.

———

"What about Lisbon?" Bex asked the day I left the infirmary. The sun was shining, and she stretched herself out on a blanket by the lake, closed her eyes, then bolted upright again. "Oooh …Geneva! My mom loves Geneva, Cam. I bet we can get my parents to—"

"Geneva for what?" I asked, trying to sit down beside her. My pride hurt as much as my body when Macey took my good arm and helped me to the ground.

"For this summer, silly," Liz said.

Summer…I stared blankly at the lake. I'd totally forgotten about summer.

"I go to the ranch in summer," I said, as if they didn't know that.

"Well, see, Cam. I heard my mom talking to your mom about it, and—"

"It's too dangerous," I finished for her.

It was sunny there by the lake, and yet a shadow seemed to fall across my best friends' faces.

"Mom and Dad are going to help," Bex blurted. "Just like winter break. And your mom too. And…it'll be fun."

"I don't know…It sounds…" Risky. Dangerous. Deadly. "I don't want you to give up your break for me."

"Are you kidding?" Macey asked. "It'll be great. Hey, what about my parents' ski house in Austria? The place is a fortress." Macey crossed her long legs.

"Thanks, Macey, but—"

"No. Seriously. It is an *actual* fortress. In the Alps. No way the Circle gets you there."

They sounded so confident—so sure. It was the prettiest day we'd had in weeks, and practically the entire school was outside, rowing across the lake, jogging through the woods, or, like us, lying on blankets, studying in the sun. Fresh air filled my lungs, and I could almost forget about the smoke and the tombs. Almost.

"Oooh," Bex said. "He *appears*." As she pointed across the grounds, she made it sound as if Zach's presence at the school was less *visiting student* and more *ghost*. Watching him walk through the woods, far out of earshot of the passing girls, I could easily see why.

His hands were in his pockets. His head was down. He seemed paler somehow.

"So…" I started slowly, "how is he?"

Macey shrugged. "We don't know. We hardly see him."

Bex looked at me. "How should he be?"

But I just stared off in the distance, thinking about all the things I did not know.

* * *

The Sunday of finals week, I woke up early and crept out of the suite, leaving my roommates sleeping as I softly closed the door.

The halls were empty. A heavy dew was on the grass, and as the sun rose, it cast a sort of rainbow across the grounds. The world was beautiful and quiet and seemed utterly at peace as I climbed the stairs to the infirmary and pushed open Joe Solomon's door.

The machines still beeped and buzzed, but the bandages were fewer. The bruises seemed to have faded. Fresh flowers sat in a vase on the table, but the biggest change was the fact that, this time, my mother sat in the chair beside his bed. Her head rested on his pillow. Her fingers were laced with his as they both slept—both waiting for my teacher to come home.

It felt like I was spying on my mother (and not in the cool covert sense of the word), so I was easing back toward the door, trying to slip silently into the hall, when I ran into something tall, broad, and strong.

"Oops!"

"Sorry," Zach blurted. He gripped my shoulders gently as if to keep me upright. We hadn't spoken—hadn't touched—in weeks. Standing there, I felt like we were still in the tombs, the walls closing in around us.

"I didn't see you. . . . Sorry," I blurted dumbly, then turned and ran away.

Zach found me with the pigeons.

Someone must have erased the boards, because Mr.

Solomon's code was gone and I was alone, looking out across the countryside, staring across the grounds.

I didn't turn when I heard him. I just said, "He should be awake by now, shouldn't he? He's never going to wake up."

"Of course he is."

"This is never going to be over."

"Of course it is."

"This is—"

"Cammie, listen to me. Don't talk—listen." There was fear his eyes. "This isn't going to stop on its own. It's not going away. We can't stay here—we can't *hide* forever."

"She's your mother?" I asked the question that had been burning inside of me for weeks.

"I'm sorry, Cam. I—"

"You could have told me."

"No." He shook his head. "I couldn't. I couldn't lose the one person who didn't see *her* when they looked at me. I couldn't lose that."

"Is my father alive, Zach?"

"I don't know."

"She said he is."

Zach studied me. "She lies."

"We should be dead," I said after what felt like forever.

"I know."

He stood beside me, inches away. And yet we didn't touch. A charge coursed between us like a wire, a spark. We had already seen our share of fire.

"Mr. Solomon isn't waking up," I said.

"We don't know that."

"Why does everyone get hurt but me?"

"And me," he said. He tried to laugh but faltered.

"I can't go to Nebraska this summer. It's not safe for Grandma and Grandpa to be near me." I ran my hand against the cold stone of the ledge. It crept dangerously close to his, and I whispered, "I'm not safe."

"Where will you go?" He eased closer.

"I don't know."

"What will you do?"

I shook my head, found that his shoulder was so close I wanted to rest there, but I didn't dare. "I don't know."

And then his arms were around me. When he kissed me it was hungrier somehow, as if this moment was all we had, and we had to taste it, drink it, savor it, and not waste a single drop.

"Run away with me." Zach's breath was heavy and warm against my face. I didn't hear the words, I only knew that the kiss was real—the kiss was safe.

I kissed him again.

"Gallagher Girl," he said, pulling back, holding my face in both of his hands, "we can go. We can run. We can get off the grid and stay off the grid until it's safe. For everyone." His eyes were inches from mine as he whispered, "We can keep each other safe."

"What are you saying, Zach?" I tried to push him away.

"We're the only two people in the world the Circle *will* think twice about killing."

"That's not funny."

"I'm not laughing." He held me closer. "You're right—no one's safe with us around. Listen to me, Cammie, we could do this. We've been training our whole lives to do this."

"I can't." I shook off the thought before it could take root somewhere inside of me. "No. No. My mother—"

"Would understand," Zach snapped. "I'm surprised she hasn't had the same idea." His hands found mine again. "If no one knows where we are, then no one can find us."

Tactically speaking, Zach was right. And yet I couldn't stop looking at him like he was crazy as he said, "We. Can. Do. This."

I felt his hands and knew they were still warm, blood was still flowing through him, he was still breathing—we both were.

We should have been dead.

Remember what I said about hope? About lies? If Zach had been talking crazy, it would have been easy to discount it, to turn and walk away.

But the truth . . . the truth—even when it comes in tiny kernels—isn't so easy to discard, so I stood with him, staring out at the morning light, trying to decide what pieces I should try to carry.

"I can't leave with you, Zach." I kissed him lightly.

He pulled me gently toward him, held me close and said, "I know."

Chapter Forty-Six

It's finals week now as I write this. Just this morning Bex was looking at me across the table in the Great Hall as I scribbled these last few words.

"What are you doing?" she asked.

"CoveOps report," I answered, and that was all I had to say. My friends know what is riding on these reports these days. They've seen the power of the words my father and Mr. Solomon wrote before we were even born. None of us will skimp on our paperwork ever again.

When we left the Grand Hall, Bex and Macey started toward the front door for P&E. Liz headed for the lab and one last experiment before the semester ends.

"Wait," I called, and the three of them stopped and looked at me.

My bruises are almost gone. My shoulder is well. Physically, I am my old self, but when my friends turned to look at me, they all smiled at me as if I might break.

"I love you guys, you know that, right?"

They looked at each other like maybe I banged my head a little harder than they'd thought.

"Cam..." Liz started toward me but I waved her away.

"I mean, school's going to be out, and no matter what happens this summer I just have to say it...I love you. It's just something I had to say."

Well, needless to say, that was followed by a lot of hugging. And some crying. And a fair amount of "I-love-you-too-ing." But, eventually, they had to let me go. Eventually, everyone does.

I was alone as I turned and started climbing the stairs to the Hall of History. With every step, I saw the last semester flashing by—Mr. Baxter staring at me through the dim lights at the Tower of London, holding my hand; Mr. Solomon pulling me onto the cold bridge; Zach gripping my shoulders and telling me to flee the tombs. With every memory, I heard one word over and over like a song.

Run.

Run.

Run.

Run. It's what people have been telling me to do all year, and now I think it's time I really listen.

This isn't something I've decided lightly. Believe me, I've been thinking about what I've got to do for weeks. I've weighed all the options, the angles, the risks. There's a chance that this won't work, of course, but the only person it can hurt is me, and that's why it must be done.

Zach was right.

They won't hurt me. It's the people *around* me who are being made to suffer. I won't drag this danger to Nebraska, no matter how many guards might go along. I can't stay here. This place I love has started to feel like a prison—like a tower. Besides, I'm a Gallagher Girl: I couldn't be a raven if I tried.

Zach was right.

Sometimes all an operative can do is run and not look back. Sometimes, when you're a chameleon, all you can do is hide. And so that's what I'm going to do. Starting now.

I'm going to leave this report in the Hall of History, on top of the case with Gilly's sword. Someone will find it there eventually, in the place where this all started.

Please don't look for me. Please don't worry. And, most of all, please don't think of this as me running away, but of me running *toward*.

Toward answers. Toward hope. Toward wherever I have to go to finish my father's mission and stop this thing, once and for all.

Zach was right.

A year ago he told me that someone knows what happened to my father. Someone knows why the Circle is chasing me.

And now...well...now I am going to sneak out of this mansion by myself one more time. Now I'm going to leave here, and spend this summer trying to find them.

I'll be back. And when I am, I promise I'll have answers.

Acknowledgments

With every book I write, I learn to appreciate the people around me more and more. I am incredibly grateful to Kristin Nelson and everyone at the Nelson Literary Agency for their constant guidance and support.

I owe a tremendous debt to Jennifer Lynn Barnes, Rose Brock, and all the Bobs for their keen eyes and excellent advice as this book went from vague idea to finished product.

The Gallagher Girls could not ask for a better home than Disney • Hyperion, and I would like to thank everyone there for their tireless work and endless devotion—especially Jennifer Besser, who will always be a Gallagher Girl in the truest sense.

And, as always, I could not do this—or anything else—without my family.